P001	Prologue
P005	**Side Story 1:** Hot like the Pot of My Soul
P039	**Side Story 2:** Dufufufu!!
P063	**Side Story 3:** Bespectacled Beaus: The Double Shotgun
P069	**Side Story 4:** *Durarara!!* True Stories: They Get Along
P073	**Side Story 5:** *Durarara!!* True Stories: They Get Along 2
P079	**Side Story 6:** *Durarara!!* x√20 The Coming-of-Age Comes at Once
P095	**Side Story 7:** Nicococo!! (*Niconico Novel* Short-Term Serial)
P129	**Side Story 8:** *Duramp!!* Avoiding Love in the Center of the World
P159	**Epilogue, or Side Story 9:** Festival Spirits

Design: Yoshihiko Kamabe

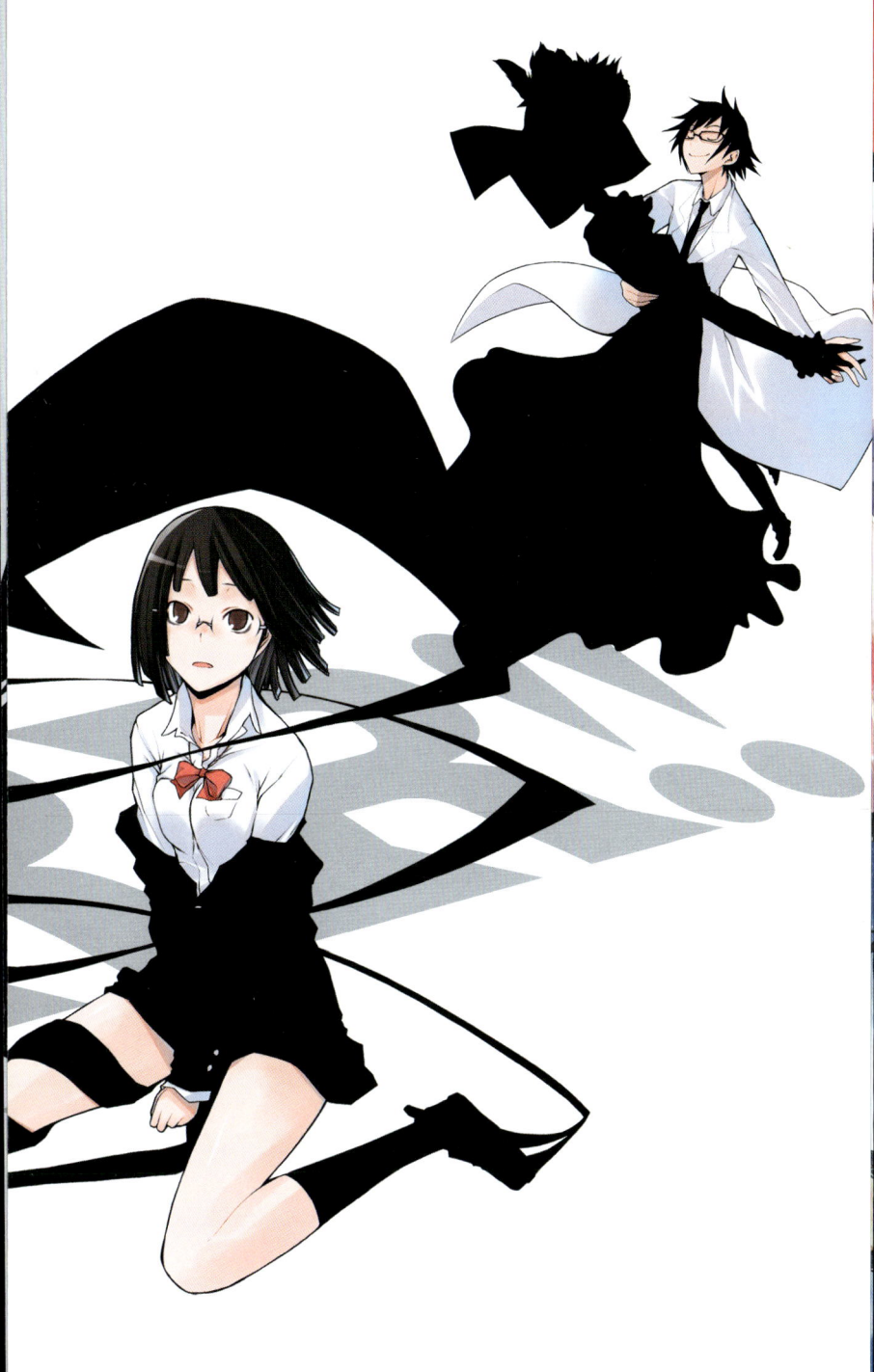

Ryohgo Narita
ILLUSTRATION BY **Suzuhito Yasuda**

NEW YORK

Durarara!! Side Stories?!

Translation by Stephen Paul
Cover art by Suzuhito Yasuda

This book is a work of fiction. Names, characters, places, and incidents are the product of the author's imagination or are used fictitiously. Any resemblance to actual events, locales, or persons, living or dead, is coincidental.

DURARARA!! GAIDEN!?
©2014 Ryohgo Narita
Edited by Dengeki Bunko
First published in Japan in 2014 by KADOKAWA CORPORATION, Tokyo.
English translation rights arranged with KADOKAWA CORPORATION, Tokyo, through TUTTLE-MORI AGENCY, INC., Tokyo.

English translation © 2024 by Yen Press, LLC

Yen Press, LLC supports the right to free expression and the value of copyright. The purpose of copyright is to encourage writers and artists to produce the creative works that enrich our culture.

The scanning, uploading, and distribution of this book without permission is a theft of the author's intellectual property. If you would like permission to use material from the book (other than for review purposes), please contact the publisher. Thank you for your support of the author's rights.

Yen On
150 West 30th Street, 19th Floor
New York, NY 10001

Visit us at yenpress.com
facebook.com/yenpress
twitter.com/yenpress
yenpress.tumblr.com
instagram.com/yenpress

First Yen On Edition: May 2024
Edited by Yen On Editorial: Anna Powers
Designed by Yen Press Design: Andy Swist, Jane Sohn

Yen On is an imprint of Yen Press, LLC.
The Yen On name and logo are trademarks of Yen Press, LLC.

The publisher is not responsible for websites (or their content) that are not owned by the publisher.

Library of Congress Cataloging-in-Publication Data

Names: Narita, Ryōgo, 1980- author. | Yasuda, Suzuhito, illustrator. | Paul, Stephen (Translator), translator.
Title: Durarara!! : side stories?! / Ryohgo Narita ; Illustration by Suzuhito Yasuda ; translation by Stephen Paul.
Other titles: Durarara!! (Light novel). English
Description: First Yen On edition. | New York, NY : Yen On, 2024.
Identifiers: LCCN 2024006742 | ISBN 9781975391188 (paperback) | ISBN 9781975391195 (ebook)
Subjects: CYAC: Fantasy. | Tokyo (Japan)—Fiction. | LCGFT: Short stories.
Classification: LCC PZ7.1.N37 Dus 2024 | DDC [Fic]—dc23
LC record available at https://lccn.loc.gov/2024006742

ISBNs: 978-1-9753-9118-8 (paperback)
978-1-9753-9119-5 (ebook)

10 9 8 7 6 5 4 3 2 1

LSC-C

Printed in the United States of America

DRRR!! SIDE STORIES?!

DURARARA!!

PROLOGUE

"The festival always feels so short when it's happening.
"But pining for its return is what allows us to truly enjoy these celebrations throughout the year."

The woman dressed in a riding suit listened to the poetic voice-over on the TV and started typing into her PDA.

"Festivals, huh…?"

"What's the matter, Celty? You look so wistful."

"I do? …How?"

The woman without a head, Celty Sturluson, could only turn to her partner and shrug her shoulders in a show of exasperation.

"I was only thinking that I've never really actively taken part in this festival thing…"

Her living partner, Shinra Kishitani, beamed and replied, "Is that right? I guess I never noticed. Every day living with you is like a festival to me."

"Well, I've passed by them on several occasions, so I know in my head what they're all about. It's just…"

She glanced briefly at the footage of the holiday crowd on the TV and continued typing, with some resignation.

"Most of the stands there are serving food, right? And I don't eat…"

"Food isn't the only draw. There are games like shooting galleries, ring toss, fishy lottery drawings, and mold carving."

"I see," Celty replied.

Shinra continued, "And nothing's quite as extravagant as the *nebuta* float parades, but plenty of localities put on their own parades and *mikoshi* shrine processions to liven things up. Some of them set up event stages where celebrities come to entertain. So there's a little something for everyone."

"*Wow, I didn't realize... What do you enjoy about festivals, Shinra?*"

"Why, seeing you dressed in a yukata, of course!" he said, eyes sparkling with delight. Celty intentionally typed out ellipses to indicate a pointed silence.

"*...............*"

But he simply ignored her cold shoulder and continued to rave about his enthusiasm for festivals.

"Every time I hear the chanting of folk songs and the sound of fireworks, I let my imagination wander. I think, how lovely would it be to one day walk through a festival with you, dressed in a beautiful yukata? We could walk behind the shrine and watch the fireworks alone, giving in to our feelings, tearing loose our garments... Which reminds me, I happen to have bought you a yukata that's sized just right to come loose off of your shoulders! Maybe you could try putting it on and then taking it *oogf!*"

She gave him a firm but casual punch to the gut, causing him to sink to his knees with a smile on his lips and a raised thumb.

"Oooh, oww... Even if you *are* the kind of heroine prone to bouts of random violence, I am more than willing to put in the work to be tough enough to take it! Look forward to next season!"

"*Was that really 'random' violence...?*"

"My real point is that I enjoy just being with you, even when it's not a festival day."

"*Okay, that may be true for you, and I appreciate you saying so, but...*"

Celty felt slightly put out, like this wasn't exactly the conversation she was hoping to have.

"And it's not just me," Shinra added. "There are plenty of people who feel more at ease being around a crowd that's there just for the heck of it. Then again, plenty of people feel the opposite, too." He reached into his pocket, pulled out his phone, and showed Celty a picture on the device. "Remember this? It wasn't any special occasion in particular, but we all had a good time, right?"

Celty felt nostalgia flood through her. "*Ah, yes... That was a fun time...*"

It was a picture of the apartment they were in right now, only with the addition of some high schoolers, a man in a bartender's vest, and a number of other casually dressed people, hanging out around a hot pot.

"I never would have guessed that Mikado would do what he did, just a few months after this…"

SIDE STORY 1: HOT LIKE THE POT OF MY SOUL

SIDE STORY 1
HOT LIKE THE POT OF MY SOUL

Apartment building, near Kawagoe Highway, mid-April

The word for "chaos" in Japanese is *konton*, which, if repeated often and fast enough, sounds like the bubbling of a merry hot pot. Which is why it's best when your hot pot is chaotic.

Who had said that, again? Somebody on a TV show.

Mikado Ryuugamine tried desperately to recall the person, but his mind wasn't sharp today.

Ummm... What's going on here, exactly?

The absolute strangeness of the scene surrounding him made his cheek twitch with alarm—but it couldn't stop his hand from picking up another piece of meat with his chopsticks and shoving it into his mouth.

Meat meat veggies meat veggies
 Meat meat veggies meat veggies
Tofu in a sesame glaze veggies in a ponzu sauce
 Meat can go all on its own if it's nice and fatty

This little quatrain popped into Mikado's head as he surveyed the scene around him.

He was surrounded by people, all focused on the hot pot in the center. And they were going to *town* on it.

* * *

It was the top-floor penthouse of a luxury apartment building by the Kawagoe Highway. The spacious dining room, which was the size of some apartments all on its own, was full of a hustle and bustle that made it seem positively cramped.

About ten people were gathered around the large table which featured two gas burners, each holding a large pot equal in size to the other.

The window nearby offered a view of Tokyo's night sky, but the steam from the pots was completely blotting it out, leaving only the conversation and chaos within the grasp of Mikado's senses.

"Ummm..."

He swallowed the piece of meat in his mouth and considered, once again, *why* he was present in such a place.

In the few days since starting his second year at Raira Academy, he had experienced the nasty feeling of nervous sweat dripping down his back too many times to count already, thanks to a variety of troubles—but when the woman at the center of that trouble had invited him to come over for a hot pot, he had found that he could not resist taking her up on the offer.

That context alone might make it sound like a romantic invitation or otherwise suspenseful event—but the woman who had invited him was currently sitting on the sofa that bordered the dining room, shoulder to shoulder with a man in a white lab coat, chatting happily.

Or at least, it *looked* like she was chatting.

In fact, the man in the white coat was talking endlessly at her. She was not saying a single word in response, because she did not even have a mouth to do so.

Mikado watched the man in the lab coat, Shinra Kishitani, talk to the headless woman, Celty Sturluson, and felt just a little bit envious.

Celty Sturluson was not human.

She was a type of fairy commonly known as a dullahan, found from Scotland to Ireland—a being that visits the homes of those close to death to inform them of their impending end.

The dullahan carried its own severed head under its arm, rode on a two-wheeled carriage called a Cóiste Bodhar pulled by a headless horse, and approached the homes of the soon-to-die. Anyone foolish enough to open the door was drenched with a basin full of blood. Thus the dullahan, like the banshee, made its name as a herald of ill fortune in European folklore.

One theory claimed that the dullahan bore a strong resemblance to the Norse Valkyrie, but Celty had no way of knowing if this was true.

It wasn't that she *didn't* know. More accurately, she just couldn't remember.

When someone back in her homeland stole her head, she lost her memories of what she was. It was the search for the faint trail of her head that had brought her here to Ikebukuro.

Now with a motorcycle instead of a headless horse and a riding suit instead of armor, she had wandered the streets of this neighborhood for decades.

But ultimately, she had not succeeded at retrieving her head, and her memories were still lost.

And she was fine with that.

As long as she could live with the human beings she loved and who accepted her, she could happily live the way she was now.

She was a headless woman who let her actions speak for her missing face, and held this strong, secret desire within her heart.

That was Celty Sturluson in a nutshell.

♂♀

Mikado had come to know the abnormal woman on a personal basis, which was why he was currently at this hot pot party—but he wasn't unique in that sense.

Quite a few other people were gathered at the apartment, which made it seem like he had been invited only because he'd happened to appear in the host's list of contacts. But the others were almost all familiar to him, so he didn't feel like the odd one out.

There was just one thing that left him lonely—another old friend who should have been here for this was not.

"……"

"Um…may I sit next to you?" said a girl's faint voice, right by his ear.

"Huh?! Oh, sure, sure! Sorry for taking this seat without asking," he replied. Most people were standing with their dishes because it was so cramped. Mikado scooted over to make room for his classmate, Anri Sonohara. "I didn't realize you were actually friends with Celty."

He knew they'd met before, but he couldn't contain his surprise when he actually saw Anri at the party.

"Karisawa and Yumasaki I understand, but even Miss Harima and Yagiri are here," he said, eyeing the couple happily poking at the pot. It made him think of another boy who wasn't here. "If only Masaomi were around…"

"Yes, I know," she replied, startling Mikado, who thought he was only talking to himself.

"Oh, s-sorry! That wasn't meant for you. I was just…," he stammered awkwardly, trying to come up with an excuse—but ultimately gave up and smiled sadly. "Anyway…it's true, I really wish Masaomi could be here," he murmured wistfully over the chatter of the room as a whole. "The only reason I know you—and everyone else in this room—is because Masaomi convinced me to move to Ikebukuro."

"……"

Masaomi Kida.

He was Mikado's childhood friend, and the very person who had invited him to Tokyo.

The three of them—Mikado, Masaomi, and Anri—were a well-known trio at Raira Academy, fast friends who were always seen together around the school.

Until an event caused Masaomi to drift away from them.

It had been over a month since then, but Mikado and Anri still hadn't gotten over it. They felt like if they looked up, they would see Masaomi tussling with someone else at the hot pot over a particularly juicy piece of meat.

But of course, there was no sign of him here.

"I'm so grateful to Masaomi. I didn't hate my hometown, but thanks to him, I've been able to step out of my comfort zone into an entirely new world. If anyone else had tried to convince me to move cities, I might not have accepted. Of course, it's a bit of an exaggeration to act like I moved across the country to get here. It was only Saitama, just up the road, but still…"

He scratched at his hair shyly. Anri smiled at him and said, "You were really good friends, weren't you?"

"Just between you and me, when I heard that Masaomi was

transferring to Tokyo, I cried. I couldn't say this to him in person, but the truth is, he saved my butt so many times...

"I always wished I could have Masaomi's energy. When he wanted to do something, he'd just do it. When we were in elementary school, there was this one time when..."

♂♀

Five years ago, summer, Saitama Prefecture

"Mikado! Let's go catch rhinoceros beetles!" said a black-haired boy with great delight, calling to an upstairs window of a two-story home.

The other boy popped his head out, dressed in his pajamas, and spoke just loud enough not to disturb the houses around them. "I wondered why a rock was hitting the window... Masaomi, do you have any idea what time it is?!"

"Two in the morning! It's the witching hour! We did it!"

"We didn't do anything! Hang on, I'll come down..."

Without changing out of his pajamas, Mikado Ryuugamine trotted down the stairs and opened the front door, sighing.

"Why rhinoceros beetles?" he asked, eyeing the other boy suspiciously.

Masaomi Kida was equipped with his bug-catching net and chuckling happily to himself. "I ran out of things to write about in my summer homework journal!"

"...Just write that nothing happened. That counts."

"That's boring! Who's gonna want to read that?!"

"Nobody. Only the teacher is going to read it—it's just a summer vacation homework assignment. We don't have to draw pictures anymore either, so it's not like you have to come up with something creative."

"*I* want to enjoy it. *I* wanna read it again when I'm older," Masaomi said, which was simply crazy.

Mikado sighed. "For one thing, my mom and dad are gonna be furious if they catch me walking around outside in the middle of the night."

"Huh? But aren't they all the way up in Aomori for a funeral?"

"...Oh, yeah. They did say something about that yesterday..."

"Anyway, it's not even the middle of the night. It's early morning. Even the trees and plants are asleep at this hour! And human beings don't have to run on a plant's schedule! C'mon, let's go and find our beetle paradise!"

♂♀

Hours later, in the forest, Saitama Prefecture

"...Let me guess: You wanted to do this because rhinoceros beetles sell for a lot of money?"

The boys still waited until around four o'clock to go into the nearby woods. Masaomi was nothing if not an active boy, and his sheer go-getter enthusiasm was not very childlike, for better or for worse—but his motivations themselves were still rather childish.

People in Masaomi's vicinity often found themselves subject to his whims; Mikado, who was particularly prone to passivity, was the most frequent victim of Masaomi's "adventures" and "ideas" and "play pretend."

Mikado did not dislike this, however. He felt something akin to admiration for the boy who got up and did things that he himself would never have tried. They were together so often that Mikado usually had a pretty good idea of whatever was driving Masaomi's latest plan.

"Hey, you figured it out. We can get some good allowance out of this."

"That's so selfish..."

But despite his misgivings, Mikado was along for the journey.

What did Masaomi's parents think of all this, anyway? He claimed that they didn't care much about the little things, but it seemed kind of weird that they would ignore the fact that their son was going out at two in the morning.

They made their way through the dark forest, Mikado jumping with fright even as he worried for his friend's home life.

"Last night, I soaked a cloth in a special kind of nectar and wrapped it around a tree. It'll be covered in beetles now, so we can take our pick. Just be careful not to step on any of 'em, got it?"

"G-got it," Mikado said, pointing his flashlight down at the space in front of his feet. The thought of accidentally squishing a bug sent a horrified shiver down his spine.

Masaomi, meanwhile, strode forth without concern. But then he saw something.

"Huh?"

Deeper into the woods, there were a number of other lights, waving and flickering.

"Th-there, see? You didn't ask if you could put that cloth up, so the adults got mad and came to take it down!"

"In the middle of the night?" Masaomi said, pointing his flashlight down and carefully following the beam.

Mikado continued following behind, despite the fear that made his knees quake.

What they found, instead, was a couple of boys who were several years older than them.

"Huh? What are you doing here?" said one of the boys, who had noticed their flashlights.

They were carrying an insect cage, too, and had come in search of rhinoceros beetles, just like Masaomi. They seemed a little too old to enjoy making them fight, so they were probably intending to sell them.

There were gobs of beetles already in their cage, and presumably they had already cleaned out the cloth of all the bugs it had attracted.

"Uh-oh, I think they're middle schoolers," Mikado whispered fearfully, pulling on Masaomi's sleeve. But his friend just spoke to the older boys like it was a totally normal situation.

"Umm, we're here to catch some rhinoceros beetles."

The middle schoolers looked at each other, then laughed and told Masaomi and Mikado, "This is where *we're* catching them. Go somewhere else, you babies."

Masaomi just sighed and turned on his heel to leave. Surprisingly, it was Mikado who jumped out from behind his friend and accosted the older boys, despite his nerves.

"B-but it was Kida who put up that cloth and the nectar!"

"Huh? What, you got a problem?"

"Oh yeah? Can you prove it?"

They shone their lights in his face and stepped forward menacingly. Mikado twitched and froze, but Masaomi grabbed his arm and pulled him away, shaking his head.

"Nope, we can't. We'll be going now."

"Yeah, you better," they laughed, waving their arms at him like they were shooing away a dog. Mikado looked upset, but Masaomi just took him by the hand and pulled him further into the woods.

"Listen, Mikado, you don't know the first thing about fighting, so you can't go around challenging people like that."

"B-but...you were the one...who lured all those beetles in...," Mikado grumbled, still not over it.

Masaomi patted him on the head and took something out of his fanny pack. "Listen, it's okay. I found lots of cool stuff in the woods here around sunset."

"Cool stuff? Like what?"

"Anyway, you're kind of a wimp, so don't go doing anything dangerous." And with a smirk, he turned to Mikado and added, "Why don't you wait here for a bit?"

"?"

"Leave the dangerous stuff like fighting up to me."

"Damn, I bet we can get tons of money with these."

"We'd probably get even more selling them to people ourselves instead of through a store, huh?"

"Don't be stupid. It's parents who buy them; nobody's gonna buy them from *us*. The best way to do it is sell them to the guy who runs the pet shop nearby."

The middle schoolers gazed greedily at the beetles in their cage, laughing over their find—until something splattered all over them.

"?!"

It was a sticky liquid that smelled rather sweet.

They cast their flashlights around, searching for the source—and saw a young boy standing alone in the darkness, holding a stick in one hand and a plastic bottle in the other.

"Hiya. Thought you might wanna take the rest of the nectar with you," he said with a mocking laugh, then turned and ran off into the night.

The older boys stood there a moment, taken aback. When they realized what had been done to them, they chased after him, roaring with fury.

"Get back here, bitch!"

"I'm gonna kick your little ass!"

They ran and ran through the darkness, issuing very immature threats to a boy who was clearly much younger than them, but just when they were getting close to catching him, the boy suddenly slowed down and swatted something hanging from a tree with the stick in his hand.

"Huh...?"

They eyed him with suspicion and shone their flashlights on the object, just as the younger boy clicked his off.

And from the object emerged the sound of many large, angry, buzzing...

"W-w-wasps!"

A great cloud of insects swarmed from the hive and found the source of their anger: a group of boys doused in nectar and waving bright lights around.

While the middle schoolers screamed and fled, Masaomi went back to the previous spot, picked up the bug cage, saved the biggest beetle, and let the others back into the forest.

Then he returned to Mikado, as though nothing out of the ordinary had just happened, and reassured his worried friend that everything was just fine.

"Sorry, I only caught this one. Do you mind if I keep it?"

♂♀

Five years later, hot pot party

"...And when I heard those older boys screaming, I knew something was up. Masaomi always hated to lose...so he would go at it with middle schoolers without thinking anything of it."

"That sounds like him," Anri chuckled. Mikado smiled back shyly.

"Yeah...but if that were all there was to him, I don't think we would have been so close. I don't like fighting, either."

♂♀

Five years earlier

Two days after the beetle incident, Mikado was walking through the neighborhood when he ran into Masaomi.

"Hey, Mikado. Check it out."

"?"

Masaomi handed him a piece of hard candy, so all he could do was say curiously, "Thank you?"

The other boy laughed at his friend's reaction and explained, "Remember how I got you up so early the other day? Well, I sold that beetle at a premium. Thought I'd share the wealth."

"So you did sell it after all," Mikado remarked, putting the candy in his pocket.

After that, they chatted a little more, and went their separate ways back home, just like any other day—if all had been normal.

But on the way back, while he was sucking on the candy Masaomi had given him, Mikado spotted some of the local kids having fun and showing off their rhinoceros beetles to each other.

He reminisced fondly about the early morning incident two days ago, but soon one of the children noticed him and waved.

"Hey, it's Mikado! What are you doing?!"

"I'm just walking home… Did you catch those beetles on your own?" he asked.

One of the kids gave him a cheeky smile and said, "No! Masaomi gave it to me!"

"…Huh?"

Mikado was startled to hear the name of the friend he'd just talked to, and he looked at the little boy more closely; he was another student at the same elementary school. The beetle in that boy's hand was clearly bigger than the others. In fact, it seemed to be exactly the same size as the one Masaomi had taken home the other morning.

"About three days ago, Yocchan was bragging about the beetle he got from the store, and everyone was really mad about it, so Masaomi said, 'I'll get you an even bigger one'!

"Then he brought me this *huge* beetle yesterday and traded it to me for three candies!"

♂♀

Five years later, hot pot party

"Masaomi's kind of dumb like that, isn't he? He'll just do things that won't get him anything, every now and then."

"I think that's wonderful," Anri said, beaming.

Mikado found a smile creeping across his lips as well. "Yeah, I agree. I think that part of Masaomi is dumb, but also really awesome. Even if he tries to act a little too cool about it."

He turned to the pot to hide the embarrassment that suddenly rose within him, but he was disappointed to find that the meat was all gone, forcing him to settle for some Chinese cabbage instead.

Suddenly, Mika Harima showed up in an adorable apron and set a large plate piled high with meat down on the table.

"Don't worry everyone, there's plenty of meat to go around. You don't have to rush!" she said with a radiant smile. Mikado couldn't help but notice how very attractive she was. Then he remembered that Anri was right behind him.

No, no, no! I'm supposed to be all-in on Sonohara, he admonished himself.

Mika Harima was Anri Sonohara's best friend.

But not knowing Mika all that well, Mikado couldn't tell if that was a real friendship or not. She had supposedly dragged Anri around with her to be the plain girl that made Mika look better, but Mikado thought that Anri was far more appealing. But maybe that impression was because he had heard about Mika through Anri first and knew that she had Seiji for a boyfriend.

She's definitely the polar opposite of Sonohara, that's for sure. Maybe both of them are using the other as a foil.

Anri was more reserved and gloomy, while Mika was so bright and cheerful she seemed to have no worries at all. They were good contrasts for each other and seemed to accentuate each other's best qualities.

In that sense, it would explain why Mika Harima's cheeriness would attract guys.

On the other hand...she's a stalker.

Mikado was aware of various aspects of Mika's personality, which truthfully made it very hard to be enticed by her good looks. And besides, he had already decided that Anri Sonohara was the only girl for him.

He stuck the piece of cabbage into his mouth, focusing on the texture to take his mind off of physical desires, and returned to Anri.

"*Mglp...*" He swallowed down the cabbage with some difficulty and asked her, "By the way, when did you first get to know Harima?"

He thought it was a natural follow-up to his earlier story about him and Masaomi when they were younger—but the answer he got was darker than he expected.

"I was...longtime friends with Mika, but we weren't really that close at the start... I was being picked on in elementary school by one of the girls in class...and it was Mika who saved me."

"......"

"After that, we started doing different things together, and the rest is what I told you earlier."

"Uh, yeah... Sorry if I dredged up anything unpleasant there," he said, bowing an awkward apology.

Anri quickly shook her head. "No, no, not at all. Sorry for bringing us down..."

Just then, the devil in question, Mika Harima, popped into the conversation. "What's going on here?" she teased. "Having a little domestic tiff?"

"M-Mika!"

"Mikado, don't go giving Anri a hard time, now! She tends to internalize things and agonize over them."

"S-sorry," he said, for some reason. Anri reached out toward him, desperate to clear up what he'd just heard.

But the combination of Mika's voice and Mikado's words brought back a very specific memory to her mind.

It was from when the two of them first met.

♂♀

Six years ago, Tokyo, elementary school

A wet rag smacked against Anri's little face.

"How'd you get a perfect score on that test? What did you do to cheat?"

"......"

She was surrounded by girls at the washing faucet behind the school building. It was after school; there were few people left around and no teachers walking nearby.

"Everyone knows you were cheating," said one of the girls, pulling the rag off of Anri's face and hurling it at the gentle swell of her chest. It made a nasty splat, leaving a wet mark that spread across her shirt.

Although Anri did not deserve it, they were apparently angry that she, one of the plainer girls in the class, had gotten better grades than them. Lacking evidence, they had simply skipped over any investigation to declare her guilty of cheating.

"But I didn't…," she tried to claim, but the leader of the pack of girls grabbed her shoulder and pushed her back against the wall of the washing area.

"I didn't ask for your life story."

She opened the faucet, then scooped some water into her hand and threw it against Anri's face several times.

"Everyone *hates* you, you know. Don't you get that?"

"Yeah. All the boys said you're gross."

As a matter of fact, the boys probably liked Anri more than they liked the girls who were picking on her, but to bring up that fact would only hurt their fragile pride even more. The realization that the "inferior" girl had beaten them badly on the test was more humiliation than they could stand, given the status they'd built within the class.

But being children, they would probably say that she just made them mad.

One of the girls filled a bucket and pulled back to hurl the water at the unresisting Anri.

But in the next moment, a hand reached out and grabbed the girl's wrist, causing her to lose her balance and spill the water on herself instead.

"Aaaaah!" she screamed, drawing the attention of Anri and the bullies. Mika was standing behind them with her backpack on, ready to walk home, along with other girls who seemed to be her friends.

Mika ripped the bucket away from the drenched girl and spun it around on her finger, smiling very wickedly to herself.

"What're you losers even doing?" she cackled, much to the distress of the bullies.

"I-it's none of your business, Harima," they said, clearly intimidated.

Mika was the central figure of the class at this point in time, and the bullies' group was an inferior rung on the hierarchy of popularity.

In fact, they were where they were because they hadn't been deemed good enough for Mika's popular group, which was why they had turned to establish their own superiority over Anri. The fact that Mika had spotted them made this a rather awkward encounter.

"Uh-oh. I wonder what the teachers would say if they heard about this. They might have to call your mommies and daddies." Mika snickered.

The bullies stammered, "D-don't get the wrong idea! We were just teasing her a little… A-anyway, let's go."

They scampered off, pale-faced. Mika laughed as they went, then turned to Anri. "You okay?"

"Um…thank you…"

"Wipe your face," she said, offering Anri a handkerchief. "Come on, Sonohara. You should at least fight back a little. Otherwise they're just going to take it further and further."

"I'm sorry…but…I'm all right… I'm *used to it* back home…"

"?"

At the time, Mika didn't understand what Anri meant by that. But it made her curious.

So she said, "We're about to go hang out. Wanna come with us?"

♂♀

For the next few years, Anri was a part of Mika's posse and often spent time with them. She wasn't really an enthusiastic member of the group, more like a bystander who'd been roped into it by Mika specifically.

Anri could tell that, to Mika, she was like a completely contrasting life-form that served to make herself look better. Being in elementary school, she was still too young to put it in those words, but she could still sense the social undercurrents at play.

But she also didn't mind it at all. Perhaps it was because, being a passive person herself, she felt a kind of allure in the way that Mika could be so proactive about everything.

Strangely enough, it was the same way that Mikado Ryuugamine felt about Masaomi Kida.

But in the spring of their second year of middle school, things changed.

* * *

"Aaah!"

The one getting kicked against the wall of the girls' bathroom was Mika Harima this time.

Surrounding her and blocking her exit were the same girls who had been the outcast group in elementary school, and behind them were the girls who had been Mika's followers back then.

"How long do you think you can play princess, huh?"

"Nobody's gonna sit around and kiss your ass anymore."

It had all started changing when one of the girls from the outcast group had started dating a boy from the gang of tough guys who ruled the school. Over time, she started testing her limits, seeing what sort of influence she could wield, and once she was satisfied, she began to take down Mika's group as revenge for her elementary school years.

Afraid of becoming targets, Mika's followers guiltily chose to change sides, one by one, until Mika was socially isolated and alone.

"Look, I brought her."

A new figure arrived at the girl's bathroom, which was tense and fraught with anger. It was Anri Sonohara, whom one of the other girls had dragged in.

"Harima…?"

Anri had been uninterested in the social competition between groups in the first place, so the change in the situation was a mystery to her.

The leader of the group jutted her chin toward Mika, handed Anri a bucket, and said, "Fill this up with water and dump it on her, Sonohara." Anri took it, but she looked back and forth between Mika and the other girls with obvious confusion.

"You didn't like being used to make her look better, right?"

"I don't mind…"

"I said, *right*? Or do you want to be picked on again? Huh? Is that right? You wanna join Mika in here and get water dumped on you every single day? Do you?"

The girls who had been Mika's friends left her because they were afraid of being the outcasts this time. And Anri had originally been the target for their bullying anyway, so the boss of their group simply assumed that she would give in out of fear of being bullied again. But…

"I won't do that."

* * *

"...What?"

They were stunned by the matter-of-fact way Anri spoke for herself.

"What would I gain?" she said.

It was such a simple question.

She wasn't speaking from a position of righteousness.

She wasn't acting out of sympathy or gratitude toward Mika.

Anri was just asking a question.

What did she stand to gain by joining them?

Maybe Anri would have made a different decision if she had faced this dilemma in elementary school. But now, having already lost her parents to a slasher's home invasion, she had built a painting frame inside of her mind that allowed her to observe her own life with an abnormal degree of objectivity.

"What's the point of associating with people like you to bully Mika?"

"You bitch..."

The others had no idea how Anri's mind worked, though, and assumed that she was mocking them. One of them pushed Anri on the chest toward one of the stall doors.

"Oh, you think you're tough, huh? Then we'll just strip you and Mika naked and take photos of you."

They were intending to take nude pictures of Mika to use as blackmail to ensure that she wouldn't tattle to the teachers about what they were doing to her. Doing the same to another person wouldn't be that big of a deal. They pinned down Mika and Anri, intending to go through with their plan.

"Oh, geez. Anri, you should know better."

From the back of the room, Mika chuckled to herself. She was holding the handle of a cleaning mop that she'd pulled out of the supply locker at the back of the bathroom. The light of the late afternoon coming through the window lit her from behind, giving her an eerie silhouette.

"Huh? What, are you trying to fight back or something?"

The girls took a step back, expecting her to start swinging at them with the mop, but they weren't intimidated.

Mika wasn't bothered by their advantage of numbers, either. "Hey, Kushigawa. The older boy you're going out with—that's Shirota, right?"

The other girl grunted. "...Yeah, that's right! So if anything happens to me, Shiro's gonna have something to say about—"

"Then the boy from the biker gang you were going out with," Mika interrupted. "Haganeda, right? You already broke up with him?"

"...?! Wha... How did you know that name...?!"

The mention of her ex-boyfriend—actually her *current boyfriend whom she was two-timing*—caught the leader of the girls by surprise, and she looked considerably less confident than before.

"You told Shirota that he was your first boyfriend, didn't you? I bet something really fun will happen if I talk to both of them about you, huh...?"

"H-h-how the hell did you find out about..."

"Oh, you don't know?" Mika said, eyeing the girl's cohorts, who had previously been a part of her own social circle. "Do you *really* think all of them have switched sides to join you? Because all I have to do is chat with them, and they'll tell me all sorts of interesting little rumors about you."

"Huh...?" The girls who had betrayed Mika gasped. They had no idea about any of this, and they had never even heard the name Haganeda before this moment. Now the girls who had always been on the new leader's side were glaring at them furiously.

"You little bitches..."

"N-no, we didn't...!"

In fact, Mika hadn't found out about Haganeda from the girls who betrayed her. She had anticipated something like this and done her own research into the group of rival girls.

It was the perfect way to make them suspicious of each other and break them apart from within—but that wasn't Mika's real intention at all.

All she needed was a few seconds. A few seconds to draw their eyes away from her.

That would be enough time for a girl with skinny arms, who hadn't dabbled in learning any kind of self-defense...

...to bring the metal part of the mop down onto the head of the girl closest to her.

There was an odd, grisly sound, and one of the girls in the rival group suddenly fell to the floor, bleeding from the head.

"Hey...!"

A different girl noticed what had happened, only a split second before the end of the mop jabbed her hard in the throat.

Stunned, the others could only watch as Mika turned to Anri and continued what she'd been saying earlier.

"Oh, geez. Anri, you really shouldn't do this."

"Huh?"

"If you start acting like such a good girl..."

The leader of the group dropped the bucket, her fingers trembling. Her followers looked ready to burst into tears. And Anri just sat there vacantly, watching the whole thing play out.

Mika gave her the most dazzling smile she possibly could, lifting the mop high overhead.

"It means that I have to be a very, very *bad* girl to play off of you."

♂♀

Present day, hot pot party

Anri smiled, reminiscing on the events of the past.

In the end, the school categorized the incident as self-defense on Mika's part.

Anri testified that the girls were going to strip them and take pictures as blackmail. Later, it was discovered that a number of other girls had already been victimized this way.

Mika and Anri continued to hang out together after that point. It might have been the first time Anri became aware of the abnormal part of Mika Harima's personality.

But Anri wasn't afraid of her. She continued to be a very good friend—or at least foil.

She was fully aware that she, too, was an abnormal person, even if you ignored the whispering voices that echoed throughout her body.

While Anri reminisced about the past, Mika continued to tease Mikado, until Seiji eventually joined in. Mikado had no choice but to look around desperately for help. Unfortunately for him, the only ones who noticed were Karisawa and Yumasaki, who joined in on the fun.

"Aww, what's wrong, Mikapon? Are you discovering the pleasures of being told off by women?"

"Don't worry. We're both hooked on two dimensions, so we'll accept you for just about any kinks you pick up."

"What are you talking about?!" Mikado exclaimed.

Seiji seemed stunned by the accusation. "Is that true, Ryuugamine? Are you into Mika, too…?"

"No, no! Don't worry! She and you are completely in love! There's no room for me anywhere in there! Does that satisfy you?!"

"Look, don't get it mixed up. I don't love Mika—I love Mika's face."

"Whaaaat?!"

"Aww, Seiji…you're so sweet. ☆"

"Whaaaaaaaaaat?!"

Mikado was so busy screaming that he was missing out on chances to grab more pieces of meat from the pot. In the meantime, two figures were busy poking at the best morsels.

One was Kadota, sans his usual beanie but otherwise the same as ever, and Shizuo Heiwajima, who was dressed the same way anyone had ever seen him.

Kadota examined the bizarre combination of prim bartender's vest and hot pot before him and set down his chopsticks. "Do you get along with Mr. Tanaka, Shizuo?"

"Huh…? Oh, you mean Tom?"

These two had been classmates once, but they didn't interact much at the time. Oddly enough, they'd been around each other more often after graduating from school.

Shizuo didn't really have anyone to talk to at this party aside from Kadota and Shinra, and Shinra had been talking nonstop with Celty, so naturally that meant the two former classmates were sitting together.

"I mean, Tom's a good guy. I owe the boss a whole lot too. I think I'm stickin' around at this job for a while. And I mean…if I don't, I can't pay back what I owe."

"Oh, yeah…all those signposts and shit that you busted up, your boss paid to replace, huh?"

"Yeah, and he pays me a salary on top of that, so I gotta admit I'm extremely grateful to him."

"Did you know Mr. Tanaka before that?" Kadota asked. He seemed oddly interested in Shizuo's bosses, although maybe it was just a topic at hand to chat about while he digested. He had a certain kind of admiration for Tom Tanaka and his ability to work with Shizuo for so long.

"Hmm? Ah, yeah, I guess so."

"I mean, the whole reason I bleached my hair is because Tom told me to."

♂♀

Ten years ago, Raijin North Middle School, Ikebukuro

"I told you…I hate violence!" insisted Shizuo, then a middle school student, in the throes of a particularly extreme bout of violence on his surroundings.

Young Shizuo swung a twisted street sign, smashing it through the upperclassmen of his new school, one after the other.

It was hard to believe that such strength belonged to a boy who had been in elementary school just a month ago. Now he was clobbering much older kids, knocking them off their feet.

The gust of violence passed very quickly, though, leaving a silence to fill the void. Between ten and twenty upperclassmen lay prone on the ground, completely unconscious.

Some minutes after that, Shizuo's anger had finally calmed, and he was ready to go home—when a man made his presence known.

"Well? Feeling any better now?"

Based on his clothes, he was a student at the same school. Based on his looks and demeanor, he was probably an upperclassman. Shizuo lifted the street sign again, prepared to continue fighting.

"Whoa, whoa, hold on. I'm not tryin' to fight you," the older boy said.

With some consternation, Shizuo decided to put the sign down. "What, you aren't here to get revenge for them?"

"I work smarter, not harder," said the older boy, who wore glasses and seemed quite grown-up compared to the childish Shizuo. "Plus… they talked a bunch of shit to you, started a fight, and got their asses beat, right? Makes no sense to take revenge for something they earned."

"……"

"I don't wanna get hurt, either," he also admitted, smirking. The older boy examined the fallen students, noted a couple that had particularly heavy injuries, and picked one up to carry on his shoulder. "Hey, would you mind helping me take them to the hospital?"

"…Why me?"

But rather than accusing Shizuo of being excessive, the older boy was practical about it. He thought for a moment, then came up with a suggestion that Shizuo had no choice but to accept.

"C'mon, I'll buy you some food."

♂♀

One hour later, cheap diner, Ikebukuro

"Sorry for making you help me."

"…It's cool."

"I don't think they'll be messing with you anytime soon. So cut 'em a break, okay?"

"It's fine. I don't care," Shizuo said, fixing the other guy with a look while he stuffed himself with milk and miso-glazed mackerel.

The other guy was named Tanaka, and he had already finished his chicken and egg *oyakodon* bowl. He was observing Shizuo's eating habits with some distaste.

"Damn, you drink a lot of milk… It's kind of weird that this place serves it by the bottle, too, though," he said, eyeing the half a dozen empty bottles on the table. "So you don't like fighting, huh?"

"…How did you know that?"

"…Dude, you were screaming about how much you hate violence."

"Oh, right…" Shizuo stirred up the rest of his food with embarrassment, then chugged the rest of the milk bottle in one go. He set it down on the table and said sadly, "I don't *want* to fight. But when I get mad, I just can't control myself anymore…and the next thing I know, I'm like…that."

"…Huh. In that case, you might as well just get it out of your system."

"Huh?"

"Let them talk about how nobody should ever mess with you, and people will stop doing it. Sure, you might get some idiots with a death wish. And if you don't want the bad reputation, getting it out of your system's not an option anyway. If you went around starting fights with everyone, you'd probably end up getting killed by yakuza eventually, but you don't seem like the type."

Tanaka took a sip from his water and glanced at Shizuo's hair.

"Maybe you should try dyeing your hair. You seem like a really normal guy as it is, so maybe that makes you an easier target. Plus, you need some easily identifiable traits. If the rumors get around about you, some folks could still try picking on you without knowing. Once people are talking about how you should never mess with the blond guy in the Raijin North Middle School uniform, your life'll be a whole lot better."

"...Man, I don't wanna go through the hassle. Plus, I got this hair from my mom and dad. I can't go bleaching all the color out of it," Shizuo said, averting his eyes.

Tanaka smirked and said, "You're surprisingly old-fashioned, huh? A real serious guy. Hey, nothing wrong with honoring the body your parents gave you. I'm not sayin' you gotta do anything. Hey, is there something that would especially piss you off if people started talkin' about it?"

"?"

Shizuo wasn't sure what he meant by that, and frowned. Tanaka chuckled awkwardly and explained, "I'm gonna be your senpai for the next year until I graduate. I just wanna know what I should avoid so I don't get my ass kicked by an underclassman." Despite witnessing the godlike violence earlier, Tanaka was willing to sum up Shizuo as simply an underclassman. "I told you, I work smarter. I don't learn as well the hard way.

"Also, you should at least watch your mouth and be polite around older students. I don't mind, personally, but it'll help cut down on a lot of unnecessary fights."

♂♀

One month later, Raijin North Middle School, rooftop

"Hey, Tom, how the hell did you tame that rabid dog, anyway?"
 "What?"

After school on a bright and sunny day, Shizuo was napping next to the water fountain around the back when he heard some upperclassmen talking by the entrance to the roof.

When he realized that Tanaka's voice was among them, his ears perked up.

"You really had it all figured out, Tom."

"You bet. All I had to do was watch you get your asses kicked and do nothing about it."

"Hey, I'm willing to let that be water under the bridge, since you got that monster under our thumb. Now the whole neighborhood is ours. If it all works out, we got nothing to fear from *high schoolers,* even. All we hafta do is manage that Heiwajima kid, and the world is our oyster."

Rage started boiling up inside of Shizuo at the things they were saying about him.

But then Tanaka—whom they called "Tom"—just sighed and verbally dumped a glass of cold water on both Shizuo and the upperclassmen.

"Are you sure you're not gettin' the wrong idea?"

"What?"

"Tame him? He's not a dog. And if you actually talked to him, you'd realize he's way more normal than you think."

"Like I give a shit. All I know is, he seems to listen to you. If you told him to, I bet he'd wreck a whole damn high school," said the other guy, who sounded like the boss of the young delinquents.

Tom just sighed even more heavily and said, "Listen…he said he hates violence. So first of all, it don't make any sense to sacrifice an underclassman to win your battles and act like you did anything… Plus it makes you look damn pathetic."

He shook his head and made to leave the rooftop. The other delinquents spat as he left and muttered under their breaths.

"Who the hell does he think he is?"

"Hey, why don't we just take out Shizuo himself? Tom's right; we ain't shit if we let a first-year have the last laugh on us."

"And how do you expect to beat him…?"

"It's easy. Just tie up Mr. Cool Guy who just left. He's the only guy that kid likes, so if we use him as a hostage, it should be easy to sneak up and whack him on the back of the head with a bat."

It was rather chilling to hear the third-years of Raijin North Middle School talk that way about the guy they'd just been talking with minutes earlier—but nowhere near as chilling as the sensation they received when they heard a cracking noise from the water fixture on the roof behind them.

And the moment they looked up, their disquieting premonition became a reality.

"Sh-Sh-Shizuo…?!"

"Who were you going to take hostage…and who were you going to hit on the head with a bat…? Huh?!"

Then he kicked one of the water tanks, *breaking it loose*—and the upperclassmen had to be hospitalized for the second time this school year.

♂♀

Months later

And after plenty of that, eventually there was an incident.

Someone who picked a fight with Shizuo decided to get revenge after losing by targeting not Shizuo, but Tanaka.

From what Shizuo found out after the fact, the delinquents had told Tanaka they'd let him go if he just called Shizuo over. Tanaka sighed and replied, "Well, he's technically my junior at school…so if he's done something wrong, I'll try to convince him to apologize. But let me guess: you guys messed with him first, right? I can't sell out a kid who didn't do anything wrong."

After that, it turned into a fight. By the time Shizuo got there, a number of the punks were on the ground, but Tanaka wasn't doing too hot, either, and he could barely stand on his own.

Once he'd thrashed the other dozen or so thugs to his personal satisfaction, Shizuo made his way over to Tanaka, who had lay down just far enough away to avoid the chaos. "Aren't you supposed to be bad at fighting?" he asked. "It's like the other guys said, you should just use me to stay out of trouble. Why didn't you do that?"

Tom Tanaka just smiled and replied, "I'm bad at fighting. That's all there is to say."

He put on the bravest face he possibly could, playing the role of the cool and collected senior, and shrugged.

"Besides, you're not just uncomfortable around violence, are you? You *hate* it. So it's better if you don't do it."

♂♀

Present day, hot pot party

"After that, I bleached my hair blond, like Tom told me to... Once the stories about me started getting around, most guys stopped picking fights with me. Things got fairly quiet for a while," Shizuo said wistfully.

Kadota nodded and murmured, "Sounds like a good mentor to have around."

"Yeah, I guess...but then we ended up in separate high schools. Once I met that fleabrain, things all went to shit again..."

Kadota noted the darkening anger spreading across Shizuo's face at the mental image of his archenemy, and quickly spoke up to divert the conversation.

"Look, take it easy. He's somewhere all by his lonesome because nobody wanted to invite him to an occasion like this. You don't have to waste your mental energy on such a loser."

"...Let's hope he takes the hint and never comes around again," Shizuo said. His rage gradually subsided as he envisioned his hated rival, Izaya Orihara, looking sad and lonely around a hot pot with no friends.

"Speaking of weird folks, how'd you get in with that bunch, Kadota? Where'd you meet them?" he continued, looking in the direction of Yumasaki and Karisawa, who were messing with the high schoolers. (Meanwhile, in the corner of the room, Togusa gaped at a brand-new picture frame and shrieked, "I-is this a Ruri Hijiribe autograph?! What is this doing here?!")

"Ah, yeah...them..."

Kadota lowered his gaze, thinking fondly on the past.

"I'm pretty sure the first time I met them was..."

♂♀

They would never forget that winter four years ago.

Kyouhei Kadota and Walker Yumasaki were students and apprentice butlers.

They were in the service school at Hakureiryou Academy High School, the bright and prospective gentlemen-in-waiting, competing to see who would serve a more elegant master.

And that was when they came across the Black Rose Queen, dressed all in black—the esteemed daughter of the Karisawa Group, Erika Beatrice Karisawa!

Kadota fell in love at first sight... Yes, he had not yet entered the service of his master, but was already a slave—nay, a butler to love!

"...Excuse me?"

But one day, Kadota realized something. The person he was today wasn't the real him. The emotion he was feeling for the young lady was not love, but respect and admiration!

And then Kadewta made the most profound realization of all. His erstwhile rival, Walker, was in fact the one in whom he could seek the greatest solace...

"...Hello?"

Wait, Karisawa, stop it! You do realize that indulging in BL fantasies about me and Kadota right in front of us is only feeding the stereotypes that people have about otaku, don't you?! I think it's clear that in this situation, I would be Kadota's avatar and romantically conquer the many girls who approach me. The situation calls for romance! In fact, forget Kadota—it's just me, and when I'm surrounded by my harem of adoring babes, my bandaged right hand itches with the power of the ancient Epimptians, and sends them into a tizzy....

"...You can stop now."

What? You were the one who started it off by claiming me and Dotachin were lady and servant, Yumacchi. What about this, then? Through some kind of mix-up, Dotachin wakes up as a girl one day and attends an all-girls dorm school...

* * *

"That's enough outta you two!"

♂♀

Right as Kadota was about to tell his story, Yumasaki and Karisawa stepped in and began to describe their obnoxious fantasies instead. He grabbed them both by the scruff of the neck to shut them up. (Meanwhile, Togusa was pestering Celty for answers: "Wh-where did you get this autograph?!")

Shizuo watched them, scratching his cheek awkwardly. He put some meat in the pot and murmured to himself.

"…Well, as long as he's enjoying himself, I guess it doesn't matter."

♂♀

"Oh, what's all this? All you young folks talking about old memories, like you've been living that long in the first place?" teased Shinra happily, observing the guests of their hot pot party. "Of course, as one familiar with the vicissitudes of life, I know it's not a bad thing to revisit memories. I may not have robbed the cradle, so to speak, but I think that it might be fun to share about an event between Celty and me that helped define our love ten years ago—that old kidnapping incident! You don't mind, do you, Celty?"

The sudden mention of a kidnapping drew the fascinated gazes of the room onto Celty…

"I told you, it just appeared in the mail for Shinra. I don't know why we have a Ruri Hijiribe autograph, either," she was explaining to Togusa, and thus hadn't heard what Shinra was saying.

But she could tell that the room had gone silent, and realized she was the center of attention, so she turned to Shinra and typed into her PDA: *"Um…what?"*

"I'm talking about the kidnapping ten years ago, where we first realized our love for each other!"

"…*What the hell are you talking about?!*"

"Whaaat?! Y-you know! It was a huge event at the time, involving politicians' schemes over the rights of the Etsusa Bridge construction! Remember that bigtime Diet member, Mr. Naramori? And you and I were both dragged into it?!" Shinra explained desperately.

This only confused Celty more. But then she said, "*Ohhh, that did happen…didn't it?*"

"*That's* all you remember about it?!"

Shinra reeled at the revelation.

Kadota patted him on the shoulder. "…Look, I don't know what happened, but not everyone feels the same way about these things. Sometimes the results can be one-sided. Especially in your case. Don't worry about it."

"N-no, you don't understand! At the time, we… Oh, I know! Izaya… Izaya Orihara would know! I'll go and call him right now, and he'll back me up on this matterghergherghergh—"

Kadota put a hand over Shinra's mouth to keep him from mentioning the name of the absent any longer. He whispered into Shinra's ear, "Do you *want* Shizuo to tear down your apartment building?"

"Mrrgh…"

Shinra recalled that the demon in bartender's clothes was still present, and sadly gave up on his idea.

Celty walked out onto the veranda alone. She watched the streets and buildings below, feeling irritation crawling up her shoulders.

He knows every idiom and fancy saying in the book…but has he never heard of "To keep your own secrets is wisdom"? This is embarrassing for you, Shinra.

She looked up into the night sky next, wistfully recalling the past, and the distant incident that occurred there.

But that is a story for another time.

♂♀

One hour later

"I'm really amazed that so many people showed up today… Um, I'm very thankful for the invitation," said Mikado to Shinra, feeling completely stuffed. Anri had just gone to the kitchen to help peel the apples for dessert.

"Well, there are people we just met and got to know today, so I suppose we can always use today's events as future memories," said Shinra, the rare piece of advice he could offer to a student from his old school.

"But it's not like anything particularly memorable happened today..."

"We had hot pot and made friends. Isn't that enough? The soft and friendly meetings are important to remember too, you know," said Shinra. He chuckled to himself, thinking of someone else, though it wasn't clear whom.

"There are people out there in the world who know nothing of such pleasant events. Solo hot pot is the best for them."

♂♀

Elsewhere at that very moment, in a Shinjuku apartment, a little sneeze echoed off the walls.

"...Maybe I caught a cold," grumbled the information broker, grabbing a tissue.

But he would not understand the full ramifications of what he had caused the other day—or the wonderful, pleasant hot pot party he had been completely shut out of—until later.

Just half a day in the future, however...

"Let's see...what shall I do next...?"

Even that gloating, villanous line felt strangely empty and lonely today, for some reason. Nevertheless, the information broker forged ahead on his keyboard.

The man with no human connections he could truly trust sat alone, typing away.

Tappa-tappa tappa-tappa tappa-tappa click

Fin

INTERMISSION A

"*I have to say, the last few years have truly been the year of upheaval...*"

"Agreed. Although I'm not sure how I feel about expressing a period of multiple years as 'the year of upheaval'—singular—I will admit that every day of waiting for you to come home is like a thousand autumns to me, so I suppose whether it's one year or several is a trivial matter."

"*Shut up,*" Celty snapped, opening her laptop and flipping through her collection of digital photos. "*I know it's only been a few months since all the uproar over my head, but it all seems like it was in the distant past now.*"

"That's true. My injuries have healed up, too. It's like it was all a very long dream. But don't worry, Celty—the memories of our passionate romance are all real. In fact, they're still ongoing—in the progressive tense!" he said with a smile.

Celty, however, was aware that Shinra's leg was far from fully healed, and there was a possibility that he might deal with discomfort and the inability to run at full speed for a long time after this.

"*I see. Well, don't overdo it.*"

She felt a pang of guilt that his rosy description was meant to shield her from criticism. But he was easily able to see right through her.

"That's a very kind thing to say, Celty... You're not an impostor, are you?"

"*So this is the reaction I get for saying something nice to you for once.*"

"I'm only kidding. Of course I would be able to tell you apart from your impostor!"

"*Your confidence doesn't inspire me,*" she said, annoyed but relaxed. Shinra seemed happy with the effect of his words.

"Anyway, there were several cases of impostors, weren't there?"

"*Ah, yes. The whole land development controversy involving Miyoshi.*"

"And there were other times, too. I mean, you have such a memorable and easily mimicked look. They just don't realize that, though they can imitate your clothing, they cannot imitate the appeal that oozes out of every fiber of your being!"

"*Stop being embarrassing,*" she said, lightly bopping him with her fists. Shinra accepted her blows with a smile. Then he was reminded of something.

"Oh, right, there was that Shizuo impostor, too."

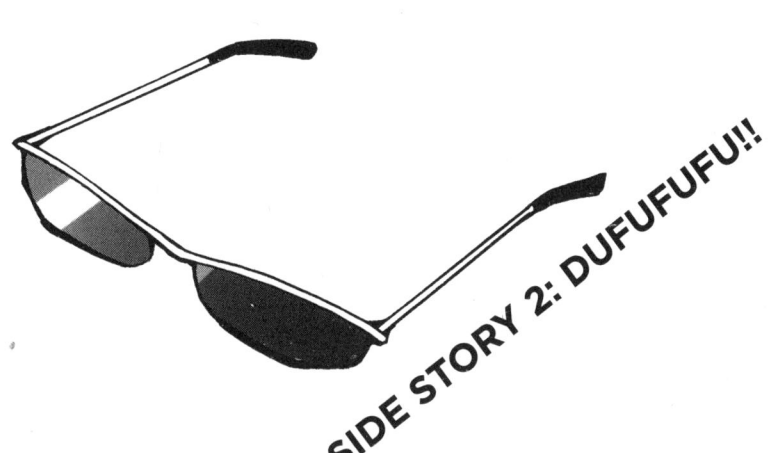

SIDE STORY 2
DUFUFUFU!!

On a certain month and date, midday, Ikebukuro

"This is the era of the impostor, Kadota!"

The beady-eyed half-Japanese young man, Yumasaki, suddenly spoke up while the van was headed down the national route.

"...So you finally say something that isn't about manga or anime, and *that's* what you choose to start with?" sighed Kadota, the man in the passenger seat.

The woman in the back, Karisawa, replied, "They're doing this impostor exhibition for a summer event right now! It's where they display robots that have very similar names to super-famous robot anime, or rip-offs of famous art!"

"That sounds...pretty dodgy, in a variety of ways."

"And here's the thing, Kadota! There was a rip-off of the *Dengeki Bunko Fighting Climax* fighting game called *Dengeki Bungo Writing Syntax*, and the staff of the original are going to redo the opening animation and exhibit it for a crowd. Even the voice actors will be there! Tonight!"

"And not only that! Every person who shows up gets a random bonus poster!"

"So it *is* about some manga or anime," Kadota groaned.

Yumasaki waggled a finger and clicked his tongue. "Tsk, tsk! It is *not*! It's a video game!"

"I don't care!"

So it was the usual nonsense from the group—until it was interrupted by an incoming call on Kadota's phone.

"Hmm? Yo…it's me. What's up?" he asked, his voice lower and more serious, so Yumasaki and Karisawa began to whisper to each other instead.

"Speaking of voice actor impostors, Kadota has a really cool voice, so I bet he could do some mean impressions if he wanted to."

"Ohh! I totally agree! He could totally do the male version of Kugen from *Our Home's Fox Deity*, or Kyosuke from *Oreimo*!"

"Ooh, and I'd love to see him put his hand on a pretty woman's shoulder and say, 'Well done, Miyuki'!"

"Yeah! *The Irregular at Magic High School*!"

They continued getting carried away and talking about irregular students and weeds, which got Kadota to wondering, *Why are they suddenly calling me a plant?* But then he realized that it was probably just another anime he didn't know about, and that it was best to ignore them and assume they were chanting Buddhist mantras or something instead.

The excitable pair continued to chatter on about the voices of people they knew.

"Speaking of similar voices, when Shizuo's in his calmer mood, he reminds me of—" Yumasaki started to say, just as he looked out the window at the sidewalk. "Oh, speak of the devil. There's Shizuo."

"What, really?"

The van was at a red light, giving them a chance to check out the people walking past. One of them was a tall man in a bartender's vest. Karisawa grinned and was going to join in on the fun when she realized something.

"…Huh? Wait, that's not Shizu-Shizu!"

"Wha?" Yumasaki took another look out the window. "W-wait, really? You're right. He's even got the bleached blond hair, too."

"Shizu-Shizu doesn't have that super-jacked pro-wrestler build. So what's that guy doing? Shizu-Shizu cosplay?"

"…Well, Shizuo is pretty superhuman in certain ways. Maybe some anime company heard the stories about him and started up their own animated version…but if it's far enough along that people would be cosplaying him, there's no way you or I wouldn't know about it… u-unless we've time traveled into the future!"

"A future where Shizu-Shizu is an anime character?! That rules! Have we finally awakened?!"

Meanwhile, Kadota's call had wrapped up. "Yeah," he said, "I wish you *would* wake up."

And Togusa, who had been driving in silence the whole time, added, "Just use your heads. He's clearly just a bartender who walked outside on his break."

The light turned green, and Togusa drove the van away from the man in the bartender's vest.

Yumasaki watched the wrestler-sized bartender go and said sadly, "Alas, the entrance to the abnormal grows distant…"

"Entrance to the abnormal, my ass. You've eaten dinner in the apartment of the Headless Rider. You're already in the realm of the abnormal," Kadota snapped.

This reminded Yumasaki of something, and he smacked a fist into his palm. "Yeah, that was crazy. I can't believe that the Headless Rider's roommate was the black-market doctor who went to the same school as you!"

"Yeah, yeah! It almost made me wonder if it was even the real Headless Rider at first!"

"And there was that period where a Celty impostor was riding around…ohhh!" Yumasaki exclaimed, coming to a realization. "Th-then maybe that person a moment ago was a Shizuo impostor! As evidence, his hair was a golden blond!"

"…Shizuo's hair is also golden blond," Kadota snapped, before he could stop himself.

"Yes, if he had a yellow scarf, then it would have been perfect," nodded Karisawa. "But there's no way that it would be a Shizu-Shizu impersonator."

"You don't know that," argued Kadota, to their surprise. He was fiddling with his phone. "That call I got earlier… What do you suppose it was about?"

"I dunno, what?"

"Some people were pretending to be that motorcycle gang, Jan-Jaka-Jan, out around Shinjuku. But then the real gang showed up and destroyed 'em."

Jan-Jaka-Jan was the name of a gang that roamed around a piece of Tokyo. Many of the members wore black suits like hosts from a host club, which made them fairly easy to imitate, if that's what you wanted to do.

The crucial point, however, was that you would have to be truly foolhardy to do that, because it was commonly known that this gang happened to have the backing of a group of grown-up hooligans known as the Awakusu-kai.

"Bunch of idiots. You should know that stealing their name and stirring up trouble is going to go right into the ear of the real thing in this day and age," Kadota grumbled, messing with his phone. Then he looked up and said, "But anyway, they definitely wouldn't do that with Shizuo."

Yumasaki and Karisawa glanced at one another and chuckled.

"Of course not."

"I mean, they'd have to have a death wish to do something like that."

♂♀

But the world is always bigger than people think.

The man in the bartender's outfit walking through Ikebukuro was, in fact, an impostor passing himself off as Shizuo Heiwajima.

"It can't be this easy." The fake Shizuo smirked as he strolled down the sidewalk.

His name was Shizuo Nobusuma.

He was your average young ruffian, lazily and unseriously working a bartending gig and following his sly and crafty whims. In short, rather typical.

This was just your average hooligan from the neighborhood of Numabukuro in Nakano Ward, but to explain why he was passing himself off as Shizuo Heiwajima, that will require going back several days.

He had just finished up a shift of bartending, and he was going with his coworkers to take the trash out before he changed out of his work duds. At that moment, there just so happened to be a fight between thugs in the back alley. He watched them, wondering if he might be able to steal the wallet of whoever got knocked out, when…

"Hey! What do you bitches think you're lookin' at?! You want some of this?!" shouted the man who had just won the fight, pulling out a knife and waving it meaningfully.

"C-c-c'mon, Shizuo, let's go," said one of his coworkers, who had already changed into his street clothes.

"Sh-Shizuo?! Shizuo Heiwajima?!"

Even the guy who had lost jumped to his feet, wide-eyed, and exclaimed, "I thought Shizuo Heiwajima was in Ikebukuro…"

"Dammit! So he's from Numabukuro, not Ikebukuro?!"

They wailed about how sorry they were for bothering him and ran for their lives.

Shizuo, completely baffled, tried to find out what it was that they were talking about. He learned that over in Ikebukuro, there was some blond guy named Shizuo Heiwajima who was famous for fighting, and he had become kind of an urban legend.

The stories about throwing vending machines and kicking cars over were obviously just stories that had grown in the telling, but it was definitely true that everyone was afraid of the guy.

Nobusuma wasn't able to find any photos, but the stories said that Heiwajima had blond hair, sunglasses, and a bartender's getup. Suddenly, he realized how the misunderstanding had happened, and an idea occurred to him.

Y'know, one of my old bros over in Shinjuku said he's been livin' the high life by passing himself off as a part of this Jan-Jaka-Jan gang. Maybe I could get in on this game on my own!

And without thinking much of it, he bleached his hair blond and headed over to Ikebukuro.

"Damn, the stories really are gettin' around, huh?"

Shizuo had stolen an outfit from work, put on a pair of shades, and walked around a bit to see what would happen.

"Eeek!!"

"Whoa…"

Simply walking around earned him frightened glances from locals, who hurriedly backed away from him. Not all of them, of course, but every kid who looked a little on the rough side was staring at him in terror.

This is wild. Damn, the stories of this Shizuo Heiwajima guy must be everywhere around here. I figured that people would know his face better, but he's more of an urban legend. All they know are the broad rumors.

Or maybe the resemblance is even stronger than I thought.

He was already the size of a professional wrestler, and if he dressed a little on the tough side, people would naturally make way for him, but he had *never* experienced such raw fear directed at him before.

And if the real thing shows up, I ain't scared.

He'd been known as a fearless fighter, so if the real Shizuo Heiwajima made an appearance, he knew he could take the guy out.

I'm just gonna steal this Shizuo guy's infamy for myself. It's too sweet to pass up. This is the shit!

Shizuo Nobusuma felt like he had turned into some kind of dictator overnight, and soon worked up the boldness to try messing with someone on the street.

Which random sucker will it be...?

Hey, what's with that pitch-black bike?

He had spotted a motorcyclist stopped on the side of the road, wearing a black jacket and checking something on a PDA.

The outfit was as black as shadow, and so was the ride itself. The bike didn't even have a license plate on it. Shizuo decided that the owner was probably just an idiot who wanted to be special.

And he had no idea that this person—the Headless Rider—was an Ikebukuro urban legend even more famous than Shizuo Heiwajima.

Even Shizuo had heard the stories about the Headless Rider, but because he didn't watch TV, he had never learned what the rider actually looked like. He also wasn't imaginitive enough to envision that he'd run across a paranormal entity smack in the middle of the day.

"Hey, pal. Real fucked-up ride you got there."

"......"

The rider just stared at him.

They seemed surprised, but they didn't say anything. The helmet tilted up and down, as if the person was trying to gauge him.

"Huh? The hell you starin' at, huh? Who said you could come here on my turf and show off? You know there's a price to be paid to the great Shizuo Heiwajima before you can ride around here, yeah? Huh?"

They were good old-fashioned fightin' words, which the biker in black accepted in silence. Then they pulled a wallet out of somewhere, removed a ten-thousand-yen bill, and held it out to Shizuo.

"…?! O-oh, cool. Yeah, that'll do," he said, not expecting it to actually work. He took the money rather anticlimactically.

Then the bike took off without a sound. He didn't notice that a motorcycle without an engine sound was completely out of the ordinary; he was too absorbed in the sizable amount of money in his hand.

Holy shit, no way! Is it really this easy?! Damn, I mean—really?! Goddamn! I shoulda asked him for more!

He headed into central Ikebukuro with a smile plastered across his face and not a thought in his mind about the overall eeriness of the situation.

He had failed to notice something important.

That all of the locals who had cried out in alarm and backed away—had then cast pitying glances at him as he walked away.

♂♀

Along Kawagoe Highway, Shinra's apartment

"A fake Shizuo?" asked the man in the white doctor's coat, Shinra Kishitani.

The Headless Rider, Celty Sturluson, typed into her PDA, *"Yeah, I actually just gave him some money."*

"Why?! He's a fake! I don't think you'd even give the real one money! I know business has been good lately, but throwing money away like that isn't even benefiting society!"

"Yeah, but…" She paused, shook her head, and then typed with great pity, *"I just feel so sorry for that guy, knowing that Shizuo's going to beat him into the ground soon… It was like an offering, or incense money for his funeral…"*

"…Why wouldn't you just tell him to stop doing this before he gets killed?" Shinra asked her, quite reasonably.

Celty typed back, *"Why do I have to be nice to someone trying to shake me down for money?"*

"…Ah. Good point," Shinra said, satisfied. He sighed.

"First he's hated, then he's pitied. This impostor really gets around."

♂♀

Back alley, Ikebukuro

"Hey. Move it, you slugs," Shizuo said, threatening a group of young men who were chatting and loitering outside of a store.

"The fuck?"

They glared at him as they turned—and promptly changed their tune the moment they saw how he was dressed. They were immediately apologetic and submissive.

"Sorry! So sorry! Greetings, Mr. Shizuo! Here, have a drink on me!"

One of the thuggish young men offered him an unopened plastic bottle. He took it and grunted, "Cool," then left, without thinking twice about the interaction.

After he left, the young men turned back to one another.

"Is that the guy they mentioned in the Dollars newsletter? The Shizuo Heiwajima impostor?"

"I can't believe someone would actually do something this stupid."

"What was that, though? 'Have a drink on me!'" laughed one of the guys.

The one who had handed the fake Shizuo the bottle replied in a very similar way to the Headless Rider's typed response.

"I mean, the guy's gonna die any moment now… I just feel so bad for him… The least thing I can do is give him one last fond memory before it happens."

♂♀

Similar scenes continued to play out after this, until Shizuo was completely beside himself with delight.

"Dufufufu… What the hell is going on? This is amazing," he muttered, smiling creepily. He prowled the area, looking for more ways to take advantage of his good fortune—but he wasn't watching where he was going and bumped right into a very tall, large back.

At first he thought it was a wall, but then it became apparent that it was indeed a person.

"Watch out, idiot! I'm Shizuo Heiwajima!" he snapped, sounding rather foolish himself. But he had left his common sense behind some time ago now and shouted without any thought that it might backfire on him.

As it turned out, the man he was accosting was larger than he was, Black, and dressed in a sushi chef's apron.

"Shizuo? Hmm...? Boss, you really Shizuo Heiwajima? Your face look different."

Holy crap! Who is this guy? Does he know the real Shizuo Heiwajima? N-no, wait. To a foreigner, all Japanese people look the same.

Completely unaware that the sushi restaurant worker, Simon Brezhnev, had known Shizuo Heiwajima for years, *this* Shizuo decided to continue his winning streak.

"Y-yeah, I put on a little weight."

"Ohh, I see. Weight is good. Big body, need lots of calories. You eat Shizuo's favorite sushi, good for you."

"Huh?"

"Tuna, abalone, sea urchin roe, caviar sushi, we bring you true flavor," the man said, a sales pitch that some might take as sarcastic, and clapped his hands on Shizuo's shoulders. He guided him into the nearby restaurant with unstoppable force.

Frightened by the man's strength, Shizuo decided that he didn't want to be outed as an impostor—ironic at this point—and allowed himself to be pushed into the sushi place.

♂♀

Thirty minutes later

"...My money..."

"Shizuo's favorite is expensive sushi," the man had said, then brought out a procession of only the priciest items on the menu, one after the other, until Shizuo's wallet was significantly lighter.

Shizuo tried to slip out without paying, but the knife-wielding cook was intimidating enough that Shizuo had no choice but to do as he said and pay the bill.

"I mean, it tasted good, but...it's not supposed to go like this," he grumbled, checking the damage to his wallet. Shizuo decided to move further away from the busy shopping area in search of someone he could take out his frustrations on.

It was then that he saw a rather curious sight further down the alley: a man on hands and knees handing over money, and another man with dreadlocks sullenly taking it from him. And behind them, with slender limbs and shockingly alluring curves, was a young white woman.

"That's half of the day's collection done," said Tom Tanaka, Shizuo Heiwajima's boss.

As he stretched, his subordinate, Vorona, was grumbling. "It is tedious. There was an absence of violence."

"Tedious? You should be grateful that the world is at peace. Shizuo's taking PTO for his grandma's funeral, so I specifically chose collection jobs that wouldn't have any of that nonsense…"

"Such a problem is absent when I am present. Against an amateur target without firearms, pacification is possible. Killing is unnecessary," Vorona said. Her violent thoughts were delivered in precise Japanese syntax, but odd vocabulary.

Tom sighed and prepared to say something in response—but he was cut off by a bold, brash voice from across the alley.

"Well, well, well! Look who's rakin' in the dough over here, eh?"

"What?"

Tom spun around and saw a bartender's vest, blond hair, and sunglasses—a very familiar combination on a completely unfamiliar man.

"…Who the hell are you?" Tom asked, baffled.

The man grinned and replied, "You think you can shake people down for cash around here, and you don't even recognize me? You got another thing comin', pal."

"Shaking people down…?"

They were only collecting unpaid debts from a phone sex service, but Tom instantly judged that it would be pointless to explain this. He gave the man a once-over.

Why is this guy doing Shizuo cosplay? he wondered.

Vorona tugged on Tom's sleeve and asked quietly, "Has this fashion mode conquered Tokyo in recent years?"

"If you're asking if that outfit is popular these days, the answer is *no*," Tom muttered back.

The fake Shizuo, annoyed that Tom and Vorona were conversing among themselves, roared, "What the hell are you talkin' about over there? Stop ignoring me! Nobody ignores the great Shizuo Heiwajima!"

Shizuo Heiwajima.

Now that he had used that particular name, Tom and Vorona couldn't help but share a look.

"Now you're gonna give me that money you just got. Also, that chick over there's gonna come with me to a hotel roo-*hoobf!*"

He couldn't even get the word out of his mouth before Vorona's toe hit him in the throat, instantly knocking the fake Shizuo unconscious.

The man flopped onto the ground, eyes rolled back into his head. Vorona stood over him, her features betraying just the tiniest bit of irritation.

"It is displeasing that you claim to be Sir Shizuo with so little strength," she spat.

Tom sighed and said, "Didn't you just say you were bored and fed up because Shizuo wasn't here?"

"Whatever you are saying is difficult to understand. I request you present a basis for your ramblings."

Aside from the absense of Shizuo, it was just like any other conversation they ever had. Tom and Vorona walked away.

They had already forgotten about the man knocked the hell out right in the middle of the street.

♂♀

Less than an hour later

"Owww... Why was I sleeping in the middle of the street...? My throat hurts, too..."

The shock of the blow had knocked the memory clean out of Shizuo's head, apparently. He did not remember the conversation with the man and woman trying to extort their victim.

Shizuo continued to wander the area, curious about the strange pain in his throat.

It's all about money, though. I need money. Gotta find some random punks to beat up for money. And better yet, the blame all lands on this Shizuo Heiwajima sap, he thought. It was the kind of simple plan that a grade-schooler would come up with.

It was at this moment that he heard a mellifluous voice behind him.

"Oooh, are you Shizuo Heiwajima?"

He spun around and saw a man who appeared to be in his early twenties. The man wore casual, comfortable clothing and grinned happily.

"I knew it! You're Shizuo! I've always been obsessed with you! This is amazing; you're *just* the way I imagined you! My name is Tsukumoya!"

"Uh, cool," Shizuo said, but he didn't know what the man was after, and that unsettled him.

Oh, crap, does he know a lot about me? Well, even if he figures it out, I can deal with this soft-looking guy...

Once he was sure that the man had no companions hanging around nearby, he came on strong. "So what the hell do you think you're doing, talkin' to me? Huh?"

"Oh, gosh. I'm hiring you for a job, of course!"

"...Job?"

"Huh? I mean, everyone knows you do jobs as hired muscle! You beat up whoever we don't like for a hundred thousand yen a head!"

Shizuo almost choked.

A hundred thousand, just for beatin' a guy up?! That's a hell of a job—he must be rolling in it! Damn, no wonder he's a legend.

This was, of course, nonsense, but Shizuo didn't know any better. He stayed cool and made sure not to miss this golden opportunity.

"Yeah, it's true that I do that...but I don't just take any old job from any old person, you understand?"

"Yes, of course. And naturally, you're wary of someone you've never met before... But to demonstrate my goodwill, I've brought you half of the amount up front. This fifty thousand is for you!"

"...!"

He handed Shizuo an envelope with something inside. He checked and found five bills, each plastered with the lucky face of Yukichi Fukuzawa.

And I'll have ten of them, just for beating a guy up...

"W-well, if you say so. I guess I could hear you out..."

The young man beamed, said, "Thank you, Shizuo!" and bowed.

Once he was facing the ground, his smile turned much more cruel.

♂♀

Evening, Tokyo

"That's him. That's my girlfriend's dad… He pushed his daughter into being a sex worker, extorts money from me—he's a real piece of shit. And even though he's not even yakuza, he carries a freakin' knife around on him!"

They peered around the corner, where the young man pointed out a middle-aged man with a thuggish "punch perm" hairstyle.

"A knife…? Does he still have it on him…?"

"Don't worry, Shizuo! I'll blind him with this spray first. Then you can rush in and wail on him!"

"Y-yeah."

This guy seems well-prepared. It all feels a little too convenient to me…but once this all gets blamed on this Shizuo guy, I'm in the clear.

He joined Tsukumoya, feeling relatively relaxed about the whole matter, as they walked up toward the man with the perm. He seemed to be waiting for someone else to arrive, so Tsukumoya snuck up with practiced ease from his blind spot. Right as the man turned toward him, Tsukumoya gave him a healthy dose of pepper spray.

Minutes later, Shizuo had easily beaten the blinded man and spat on his head as his victim groaned on the ground.

"Your luck ran out the moment you got in trouble with the great Shizuo Heiwajima," he said, making sure that the blame for his crime would be placed on someone else. He stomped on the man's head for good measure.

"Rrg…aah…Shizuo…Heiwajima…? W-why the hell would you…"

The man with the hair recognized Shizuo's name, at least, and slowly lifted his head until his blurred vision could just make out a figure in bartender's clothes.

Shizuo almost stomped on the man's head a second time—but stopped when he heard the next words out of the older fellow's mouth.

"You think…you can make an enemy out of *us*…and live to tell the tale…?"

"…?"

The mention of "us," when he was the only person present, nagged at the back of Shizuo's mind. He turned to Tsukumoya and asked, "Hey, you said this guy wasn't a yakuza…right…? Uh…"

But the moment he turned around, Tsukumoya was already gone.

"S-son of a bitch! Where's my hundred thou—?" he grumbled, looking around for his recent acquaintance.

"B-Boss!"

"What the fuck?! Hey, you!"

Distant shouts drew his attention. He could now see, running towards him from a distance, a number of men whose line of work was clearly not a part of polite society. That was when the truth finally settled in.

The man named Tsukumoya had screwed him over.

♂♀

Shizuo just barely managed to escape the men who were almost certainly mobsters. He shook his head, panting hard.

"D-damn, man… If I see that Tsukumoya guy again, I'm gonna kill him!"

He'd been tricked into waging war on the mob for a paltry fifty thousand yen. It was time to get out of this area and undo his Shizuo Heiwajima disguise.

That's what I'll do. I'll just foist all of the blame onto this Shizuo putz. But first, I need a little more money… I'll just find someone who looks reasonably well-off, beat him up, and take his cash.

The fear and other circumstances had Shizuo on a very one-track thought process. He wasn't just acting like a hooligan now; he had downgraded to "mugger."

He looked around the area and saw a sports car parking a short distance away, with a blond man in a black suit just stepping out of it now.

Holy shit, that's a top-of-the-line luxury car. Is that guy a host at a club or something? I'll take it from him…and get the hell outta this place!

"Thanks a lot for coming out all this way, Kasuka."

"Don't worry about it."

Shizuo Heiwajima stepped out of his brother's car. Their grandmother's funeral was over.

Being a formal occasion, he was wearing black mourning clothes and no sunglasses. Even the people who regularly spotted Shizuo around the area might not have recognized him right away.

"At least Dad and Mom seem well. Are you gonna be able to visit home for New Year's?"

"...Depends on my work."

They stood by the car for a moment, engaging in brotherly dialogue, but did not get far before they were interrupted.

"Hey, assholes! Who said you could park your car there?! Huh?!" roared a furious voice.

Shizuo spun around, displeased. "What..."

For one thing, they hadn't stopped in a no-parking zone. And for another, that was definitely not the phrasing of a policeman or patrol officer.

And when he saw the man, and the clothes that looked so familiar to his own usual outfit, he couldn't help but gape.

"...?!"

Excellent. He's freaked.

Mistaking shock for fear, Shizuo rushed up and grabbed the man in the black suit by the shirt, lifting him up.

"Do you have any idea what happens if you fuck with Shizuo Heiwajima?! Do you?!" he roared. He delivered a hard kick to the door of the car in an effort to intimidate his prey.

Shizuo Nobusuma was a *very lucky man.*

If not for the fact that Shizuo Heiwajima was coming home from his grandmother's funeral, trying to stay calm out of respect for her memory—and if not for the fact that Kasuka had told him just then that he didn't care about any damage to the car—the other Shizuo might have actually died.

Instead, he was merely tossed high into the air, only to wake up in a hospital bed.

♂♀

Tokyo

"Go figure that as soon as I come back to Ikebukuro, there's a Shizu impostor on the streets! It was hilarious! You just never know what's gonna happen next in life!"

"So you called yourself Tsukumoya and screwed over the impostor, huh?" Namie sighed, watching the Tsukumoya impostor—Izaya Orihara—cackle to himself.

"Yeah. The guys he beat up had been kicked out of the Awakusu-kai, but they were still using the name to do business. Since I haven't been keeping up with Mr. Shiki for a while, I thought taking them out would be a nice make-up present."

"You mean *having them* taken out by Shizuo. It wasn't your doing," Namie noted dryly.

"Yeah, that's right," Izaya said. "The impostor Tsukumoya set the impostor Shizu on the impostor Awakusu-kai, so if the impostor Awakusu-kai go after the real Shizu…see where I'm going with this? It would be perfect if they took each other out. Oh, and I heard that the real Shizu took out the impostor Shizu."

"This is too complicated. Was there any reason to pass yourself off as an impostor of this Tsukumoya person?"

"No. Just a little prank on a business competitor," he admitted.

Namie wore a rare smile and asked, "Then should I assume the person *signing up to this crossdressing contest under the name Izaya Orihara* was Tsukumoya's idea of payback?"

"Huh?"

She glanced at the laptop—which was displaying a video of Izaya in women's clothing, walking through a park.

"What is this…? I've never done anything like that before."

"It's a composite, I'm sure. But it is *very* convincing, I'll admit," she smirked.

Izaya sighed, shook his head, and said something shockingly un-self-aware.

"I can't believe he'd go this far, just for using his name a little bit… Tsukumoya's surprisingly petty."

Several weeks later, Ikebukuro

"Oh, that reminds me, I heard that the Awakusu-kai impostors attacked Shizuo and got destroyed in the process."

"Why the hell would they pick a fight with Shizuo?"
"No idea."
"By the way, Kadota. Some folks have been raising a fuss lately on the message boards, saying you mugged them. Not that anyone actually believes them."
"...? I did? Who?"

Behind Kadota and Togusa, Yumasaki and Karisawa were busy chatting about the latest manga releases. They had just walked down a side street heading for the parking lot when someone grabbed Yumasaki's collar from behind.

"Whoa! What's this?!"

The others turned around and saw a man built like a professional wrestler.

"You stupid otaku are fillin' my ears with nerd crap. You owe me money for that," the man said, for some reason.

"……"

The four of them looked at each other. Shizuo Nobusuma was wearing a beanie like Kadota. "I'm Kyouhei Kadota," he grunted. "One of the senior members of the Dollars. Either you pay me for my trouble, or I'll call down a million Dollars on your ass. What's it gonna be?"

Seconds later, Yumasaki and Karisawa exploded into raucous laughter. Shizuo demanded to know what was so funny and tried to attack—but a red-faced Kadota pounded him flat with a devastating punch.

"Ung, I'ng soggy. I gign't gnow you were ghe real guy."
"Sorry, what was that? We were too busy filling our ears with nerd crap to hear you!"
"Hey, I gotta give this guy props for his boldness, though," cackled Yumasaki and Karisawa as they dragged the tearful Shizuo into their van.
"Look, don't worry, you'll wanna hide your face with a yellow scarf after all is said and done."
"Ahhh, it's been so long since we tortured someone, hasn't it?"
"Ung, gwat? Egsguse me? Torgture?" Shizuo stammered, his face going pale.
"Just don't overdo it," Togusa warned, and posted a message on the Dollars board: *Got the Kadota impostor. Handing him over to police.* Then he wondered, "You know, when he said 'a million Dollars'...is that what people who don't know Kadota think he's like?"

"Don't even start!" shouted the red-faced Kadota. In the backseat, Shizuo began to scream.

Once again, the city of Ikebukuro buzzed with activity—genuine and impostor alike.

Fin

INTERMISSION B

"You know, it's really easy to get sucked into clicking through my picture folder like this. I like physical photo albums because they just feel different, but it's nice that you can easily sort tons of pics on a computer."

"Both albums and digital collections have their strengths and drawbacks. And both are excellent at eliciting memories."

The pair continued to look through a variety of photos.

"Oh, these are of Karisawa's group."

"That's right. I gave her my email, so she sends me photos of her cosplay group now and then. She keeps asking if I'll join."

"What's the name of her group, again? I remember that it was something very strange."

"Oh, dear, what was it?" Celty wondered, unable to remember, either.

Shinra added a more pressing question: "By the way…what cosplay would you do, Celty?"

"I don't know…the headless knight from *Sleepy Hollow, maybe?*"

"Personally, I would recommend a more orthodox uniform-style costume, like a maid or a nurse. Any uniform you wear would be like a wedding dress to me…"

"All right, all right," Celty typed, ignoring him. She continued perusing the photos. "Hmm? What's this one…?"

"Oh, that's a picture that I took. It's the promotional image at the bookstore."

"Ah…of the *nukekubi.*"

"Yes, the *nukekubi.*"

They did not elaborate further on what that meant, and because it was not a particularly fond memory for Celty, she flipped to the next picture right away.

This time, it wasn't a photo of a person, but a series of images, all of manga pages.

"*Oh…no, not these! Delete them! Let's delete them all!*"

"You can't, Celty!" Shinra said, grabbing her hand before she could remove them all.

The black-market doctor gave her a dazzling smile and pressed his case.

"We can't delete the evidence of your debut work!"

SIDE STORY 3: BESPECTACLED BEAUS: THE DOUBLE SHOTGUN

SIDE STORY 4: *DURARARA!!* TRUE STORIES: THEY GET ALONG

SIDE STORY 5: *DURARARA!!* TRUE STORIES: THEY GET ALONG 2

SIDE STORY 3
BESPECTACLED BEAUS:
THE DOUBLE SHOTGUN

Witness the movement of heaven and earth!

This is the cosplay group "Bespectacled Beaus: The Double Shotgun," a team of six girls led by the great Erika Karisawa.

But they are no mere cosplayers. In fact, they are a squad of all-female spirit exorcists formed by the Japan Spiritual Institute to dispel the swarms of ghouls and goblins that infest the world!

These brave fighters call upon the power of the sacred cloth by donning costumes to match the shapeshifting nature of the evil spirits they fight, and sometimes bewitch their foes with feminine charms as they do battle with love and passion!

And who should they encounter but a mysterious new girl!

Is Anri Sonohara friend or foe? Is she a new witch, or will she be the seventh cosplaying angel?!

Tune in next time for "The Girl with Glasses Is a Jellyfish?"

In the space between fabric and flesh, you will witness a miracle in pink.

"The end. Tachiki will do the voice-over... And that's the concept behind our group," Karisawa explained, quite satisfied with herself.

Anri looked apologetic. "Um...I'm afraid I didn't understand a word of that..."

"Don't worry about it, Sonohara. Just ignore 90 percent of whatever Karisawa says. When she explained it to me, it was a completely different backstory," said another girl, Azusa Tsutsugawa, who was cosplaying as a character with brown hair fashioned into pigtails.

They were in Karisawa's apartment.

Nearly ten girls had come together into this paradise, all of whom—aside from Anri—were members of Bespectacled Beaus: The Double Shotgun, which meant that it was a place of utter chaos. They were trying to coordinate costumes for an upcoming event, which meant they were each trying out different sets, taking them off again, and adjusting them, over and over.

Some of them would take their costume right to the sewing machine while they were in their underwear. It was such an open and unconcerned environment that Anri was feeling quite overwhelmed by it all.

And in the meantime, Karisawa had put Anri into a witch costume, much to her consternation and embarrassment. Karisawa, who was cosplaying as an all-girls academy student of some kind, clasped her shoulders.

"Wha—?!" Anri yelped, taken by surprise.

Karisawa licked her lips and said, "Hee-hee-hee, listen to the sounds you make, Anri. Well, I think it's time for you to finally choose. Would you rather be an exorcist like the rest of the good guys, or be a witch and face off against us?!"

"Um, I don't think I want to *be* either of those...," stammered Anri, who didn't really understand what she was being offered. Karisawa started running her fingers down Anri's sides. "Hyaaaa!!"

"By the way, if you pick the witch's side, then when we perform the sealing ceremony on you, we'll be slapping wet paper seals on your bare and supple skin! Don't you think that hiding the bare body behind wet *washi* paper is just the sexiest thing? Heh-heh-heh, humina humina—oww!"

"Karisawa, you're acting like an old pervert," Azusa said, delivering a karate chop before Karisawa could start ripping off Anri's clothes.

Karisawa shook her head with disappointment as she came back to her senses. "Well, it wouldn't do to leave you ravaged and spoiled, so I guess I can stop here. Wouldn't be right to do that to Mikarun."

"Mika...? Oh, you mean Ryuugamine?" Anri replied, realizing that it was a nickname for her friend, a boy from school. "I wonder what Mikado and the others are doing for summer vacation..."

"Oh, I didn't know you hadn't seen Mi-kyun recently!"

The girly chat continued, and it nearly hijacked Anri's mind and dyed her in its own color. Someone's mind was trying to put on a new set of clothes—perhaps Karisawa's, or perhaps Anri's…

But either way, the truth was in the space between fabric and flesh.

Fin

SIDE STORY 4
DURARARA!! TRUE STORIES: THEY GET ALONG

Bookstore interior, Ikebukuro

There they stood in the middle of the bookstore like alternating piano keys: a man wearing a white coat like a doctor, and a motorcycle rider in a black suit with a full helmet.

The pair stood out like a sore thumb, but to their good fortune, there were no other customers around to be distracted by them.

"So anyway, Celty, it's so strange to see you in a bookstore. Was there something that caught your eye here?" said the man in the white coat.

The rider in black said nothing.

"Say something. It's so sad when you just ignore me. They say ignorance is a sin, but if you ask me, *ignore-ance* should be one, too! Hey... Celty, are you trembling? What are you reading?"

He looked at the cover of the magazine, *Weekly Space Mysteries*. The cover story said, "The end of the world, depicted on the paintings in Warstein Castle! Japan's recession revealed as a conspiracy by black hole organisms!"

It was that very cover story she had turned to, and it caused her to shiver as she read it.

"......"

He was about to say something to the rider when a soft cloth smacked against the large helmet. They turned to see a rather grumpy-looking store employee.

"Wow, the only time I've ever seen employees whack people with dusters for reading the merchandise was in manga... Sorry, we'll buy it," said the man in the white coat to the silent employee. The motorcycle rider also bowed, then showed her companion a PDA with a message typed into the screen.

"But if we take this terrifying story home, won't the aliens come after us?"

"...You know, I've heard it said that owning certain books might get you cursed, but never in relation to aliens... Ah, yes, sir, I'm buying it righ... Huh?"

But it wasn't their reading of the magazine for free that was bothering the employee. He used the duster to point at a sign on the wall.

No full-face helmets or ski masks inside the store, it said.

"Oh, sorry! I'll take it off now!" typed the rider in black, who seemed quite flustered at the thought of the black hole organisms, whatever those were.

"Huh? Um, Celty, dear?"

Before the man in the white coat could stop her, she ripped off her helmet...

...and revealed the void underneath.

There was an eerie phenomenon known throughout Ikebukuro: The Headless Rider.

"......"

The employee's mouth was closed and his features remained blank, except for his eyes, which widened significantly.

"Celty! Celty!"

"Huh?"

"Your head! Your head!"

"...Aaaaaaah!"

It was at this point that Celty, the very Headless Rider of rumor and legend, realized that she had taken off her helmet and promptly freaked out, limbs flailing.

The employee just stared at her without comment, so she composed a brief message.

"It's a magic trick."

"......"
"...*Surpriiiise!*"

The effect wasn't quite as dramatic when delivered via text. The bookstore employee just stared at the Headless Rider.

In the end, the rider and the man in the white coat left the money for the magazine at the register and scampered off, leaving only the sullen employee behind.

A few days later, a brand-new issue of *Weekly Space Mysteries* hit storefronts. At the back of the rack, a hand-drawn poster had been placed by a very enterprising shopkeep.

Even the nukekubi *spirit monster trembles in fear at the shocking truth within!!*

When the Headless Rider found out about the sign later, comparing her to a traditional monster woman whose head could float away and move elsewhere, she grumbled, "Nukekubi...*Of all things, he had to call me a* nukekubi," and sulked herself to sleep...

But that is a story for another time.

♂♀

This is a story set in Ikebukuro.

A tale of everyday life for people like the Headless Rider and black-market doctor, or perhaps more typical residents like the bookshop employee, who aren't quite what you would expect.

Or perhaps it is a tale about love.
A story of twisted love.

Fin

SIDE STORY 5
DURARARA!! TRUE STORIES: THEY GET ALONG 2

Shinra's apartment, near Kawagoe Highway

"Let's be manga artists, Shinra."

"...Where is this coming from all of a sudden, Celty?" Shinra Kishitani was confused by his live-in partner Celty Sturluson's suggestion. What he received as an answer was a continuation of the pitch.

"Or novelists. No big difference, I guess."

"Okay, well...how about we start by not saying something that will make enemies out of all the manga artists and novelists both, huh, Celty? But don't worry; if you made an enemy out of every creative professional in the world, and the righteous flames of their hatred on the Internet spread to burn down the entire planet, leaving only you and me left alive, I would still do everything in my power to protect you."

"...What would you be protecting me from in that situation?"

"I'd hold you just like this, to protect you from the col—derblehrghbppp!"

She extended shadows from her body that twisted around Shinra's limbs after he tried to launch himself onto her, squeezing him in a deadly bear hug arrangement.

"U-uncle! Uncle! I give, Celty! My thoracic...my T6 vertebrae can't take iiit—"

"It's far too early in the day for this kind of embarrassing behavior."

Only when she noticed his mouth starting to foam did Celty heave an inward sigh and release Shinra from her grasp.

Celty Sturluson was not human.

She was a type of fairy commonly known as a dullahan, found from Scotland to Ireland—a being that visits the homes of those close to death to inform them of their impending end.

But one day she lost her head, and the quest to find her missing part brought her here, to Ikebukuro.

It had been several decades since then, and despite the vagaries of fate, she was now living in Ikebukuro and working as a courier, doing odd jobs for money.

That was Celty Sturluson in a nutshell.

"So, what's with the sudden interest in being a manga artist?" Shinra asked, rubbing his back.

Celty turned her back toward him in shame, then typed out a message on her PDA.

"I had a thought. Is it really a good thing for me to continue being an illegal courier, constantly working for the seedy underbelly of society? Perhaps it might one day bring disaster down upon you, Shinra."

"Celty, did you forget what I do for a living?" the black-market doctor chimed in.

Celty ignored him and continued. *"But if I try to get a proper job, there are only so many options for someone without a legal identity. Or a head... So I figured, why not be a manga artist or novelist, so you don't have to meet anyone face-to-face?"*

"What about meeting with your editor?"

"You can do that for me."

"What? So I'm like a body double for you?! Does that mean that by sharing one pen name, you and I will be one being, according to society?! At that point..."

"If you say, 'we might as well share one body,' I will cut you," she said, pointing several blades of shadow at Shinra, who beamed despite the cold sweat trickling down his skin.

"That's my Celty, always finishing my sentences for me... But putting that aside, do you even know how to draw?"

"I've got it covered. Already drawn it, in fact! It's an epic fantasy based on my personal experiences!"

"What?! You work fast!!"

She pulled out her completed work so that Shinra could peruse it.

"No way, it's great... This is amazing, Celty! It's well balanced between realistic and deformed styles, the characters and background are clearly set against one another, and you even used your screentones perfectly!" he exclaimed, thrilled at the high level of technical expertise on display. He read on.

"...But Celty, the manga just ends without any kind of major event or climax to pull you in. And it doesn't seem like you're going for the heartwarming slice-of-life thing, either. What's the point?"

"Isn't it incredible?! Days and days pass without any kind of crazy nonsense happening! It's the ultimate fantasy!!"

"Celty...I think you've been involved in the criminal underworld for so long, the idea of normal life is just a fantasy for you now..."

Later, he discovered that her art, rather than being made of ink and screentones, was entirely drawn with her own shadow. Because it would be difficult to recreate in print, they realized that the art wasn't usable, and she decided to switch tacks to writing novels.

Doing research on black-market doctors and the criminal underworld in pursuit of realism, she would ultimately wind up in a gun battle in peaceful Japan...

But that is a story for another time.

♂♀

This is a story set in Ikebukuro.

A tale of everyday life for people like the Headless Rider and the black-market doctor, who aren't quite what you would expect.

Or perhaps it is a tale about love.
A story of twisted love.

Fin

INTERMISSION C

"Urgh, I guess photos can also bring back embarrassing memories."

Shinra had pressured and pressured her to save the manga drawn with her own shadow, and Celty ultimately compromised by putting the files deep into several layers of subfolders.

Once that was done, she began looking through even older files. But then she realized that beyond a certain point, there wasn't any digital camera data, and she felt a sudden and surprising sense of loss.

"Umm, where'd we put that photo album?"

"Why?" Shinra asked.

Celty rifled through the shelf and typed on the PDA at the same time. *"Well, I was having so much fun reminiscing about these photos that it made me want to see pictures that are even older."*

"Oh, I can help with that! I have a twenty-year-long album of my observation of you, Celty. We can look at it together and renew our certainty of your charms! Let's stay up until the morning singing your praises, Celty!"

"How much of a narcissist do you think I am...?" she snapped, then found a photo album at the very end of the bookshelf. *"Besides, I'm not looking for pictures of myself. I've looked the exact same for ages."*

She flipped through the pages until she found a picture of a young Shinra and inwardly smiled.

"Ah, now this brings back some memories. You didn't have glasses yet."

"Aaah, no! Put it away!" Shinra exclaimed at the picture of himself just around the start of elementary school. It was a rare show of displeasure from him.

"*You were such a good, sweet kid back then.*"

"Really?! If you like it that way, I'll take off my glasses whenever you want!"

"*...And you are neither of those things now...*"

"That's just how much I've grown as an adult," he said, undeterred. "In fact, I can show you just what a manly mature man I've become! We can start by performing some mature-audiences-only activi-terblherlbrbg!"

"*You wish you could be described as 'mature,'*" Celty snapped, holding Shinra's face in her palm before he could leap on her. "*Remember how you made a total mess of your year's coming-of-age ceremony?*"

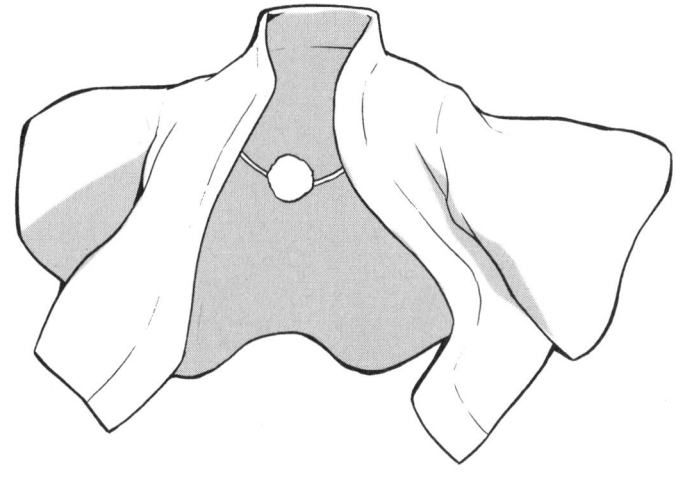

SIDE STORY 6: *DURARARA!!* X√20
THE COMING-OF-AGE COMES AT ONCE

SIDE STORY 6
DURARARA!! X$\sqrt{20}$
THE COMING-OF-AGE COMES AT ONCE

Ikebukuro, a different month and year

"Hooray! It's the twentieth anniversary of the Dengeki Bunko line!" shouted Yumasaki, out of nowhere.

"Yaaay!" Karisawa applauded.

While they celebrated inside the van, Kadota and Togusa stared at each other in the front seat, then asked the two behind them, "Uh… why are you talking about this all of a sudden?"

"It's not out of nowhere! This Dengeki Bunko anniversary has been twenty years in the making!"

"That's right, it started two decades ago!"

"Um…weren't you talking about the twentieth something-or-other last year…?" Kadota wondered, confused.

"You're wrong, Dotachin!" Karisawa said. "Last year was the Dengeki Twenty-Year Festival! This is the Dengeki *Bunko* twentieth anniversary!"

"…It is?"

"The Dengeki brand was formed at the founding of Media Works twenty-one years ago! But Dengeki Bunko was created in the June of the following year!"

"That's right. And between *Crystania* and *Gokudo the Adventurer Gaiden*, they were stacked with notable titles from the word go!" Yumasaki explained, not that it meant anything to Kadota.

"…If that's their founding lineup, why is it named like a side story?"

"What?! You need us to explain that to you?!"

"It's a long story."

"Nah, I'm good," said Kadota quickly, trying to change the topic. "Well, anyway, it's pretty remarkable that it's been going for twenty years. If it were a person, it'd be ready for a coming-of-age ceremony."

"That's right. Which is why we're going to the Sunshine Building today to check out the Great Dengeki Bunko Exhibit, which is basically the coming-of-age ceremony of Dengeki Bunko!"

"Wha…!" Togusa had not heard a word of this ahead of time. "You told me to bring the van around to pick you up…for *this*?"

Karisawa and Yumasaki ignored his pointed glare and happily said, "The next Dengeki coming-of-age ceremony is the fall event!"

"We gotta start saving up for all the merch we're gonna buy."

"Gosh, twenty years go by quick. Twenty years ago, I was barely even able to read a manga."

After a while of traveling down memory lane, Karisawa had an idea.

"By the way, Dotachin," she asked, "what was your coming-of-age ceremony like?"

"Huh…? Mine?" Suddenly his expression darkened. "I, uh…I dunno… It definitely did contain a lifetime of memories, I guess…"

The very obvious way he was avoiding the question was intriguing to the others in the van. Their gazes bored into his skin until Kadota realized that he wasn't going to be able to stonewall them. At last, he began to speak.

"Well, I mean… If it's my coming-of-age ceremony…

"…then it's also Shizuo and Izaya's coming-of-age ceremony, isn't it…?"

♂♀

Years earlier, January

This year's ceremony, which would be held in Toshima Ward, already had a disquieting air before it had even begun.

Shizuo Heiwajima, age nineteen.

Izaya Orihara, age twenty.

Because Shizuo would turn twenty on January 28, this was the year that he would come of age, too.

Of course, the likelihood that both of them would show up to attend the same ceremony was very slim. But it was not zero. There *was* a chance that they might both come to the same place at the same time.

Many who had graduated from Raijin High thought back on that time and shivered. Some of the guys who had been hardened delinquents at the time even chose to skip the ceremony out of fear of Shizuo.

There happened to be *one* graduate of Raijin who did not take the hint at all. Smiling, he called up one of his few friends on the phone.

"Hi there, Shizuo. What are you wearing to the coming-of-age ceremony tomorrow?" Shinra Kishitani asked.

On the other end, Shizuo Heiwajima replied brusquely, "What? I'm not going to that."

"No, no, you can't be that antisocial. Look, you got fired again, so you don't have anything else to do, right? It's a good opportunity to reassess how you've reached adulthood, growing from beast to man."

"All right. I'll show up tomorrow just so I can kick your ass."

"Suit yourself, but what's your plan? A formal *montsuki* hakama? Or a suit?" Shinra teased. It was easier to do that over the phone. He didn't seem to think that there was the slightest chance that Shizuo would actually beat him up tomorrow, or whenever they met next.

"See you tomorrow outside the Metropolitan Theatre when the doors open, then!"

"Hey, wait! I didn't say I was…"

Shinra hung up before Shizuo could finish his sentence, and promptly started entering another number.

"Hi there, Orihara. Are you doing well?"

"I was, until three seconds ago."

"Why, you almost make it sound like you stopped doing well the moment I called you."

"Not almost. I believe I was making the point quite clear," Izaya said.

Shinra smiled gracefully, beaming into the phone. "So, what are you wearing tomorrow? *Montsuki* hakama? Suit? Full set of armor, perhaps?"

"Were you going to listen to a word I said?"

"Oh, I did. I just ignored all of it. You do that all the time, don't you?" said Shinra without a hint of shame. "So! See you tomorrow outside the Metropolitan Theatre when the doors open, then!"

"What's this? Did I say a word about—"

Again, he ended the call without letting his conversation partner finish their thought. Then he turned to his living partner and said, "What do you think is better, Celty? A *montsuki* hakama or a tailcoat? Or—I know! Maybe I should just go wearing this white coat, eh?"

His roommate sat up slowly and typed into her PDA, *"I don't care."*

"Thank you for saying that anything looks good on me! But I think *you'd* look better in a variety of clothing than I would, Celty!"

"Why do you say that?" she typed with apparent exhaustion, though she didn't sigh.

She couldn't, even if she'd wanted to.

His roommate, Celty Sturluson, was not human.

She was a type of fairy commonly known as a dullahan, found from Scotland to Ireland—a being that visits the homes of those close to death to inform them of their impending end.

(*et cetera*)

When someone back in her homeland stole her head, she lost her memories of what she was. It was the search for the faint trail of her head that had brought her here to Ikebukuro.

Now with a motorcycle instead of a headless horse and a riding suit instead of armor, she had wandered the streets of this neighborhood for over fifteen years.

But ultimately, she had not succeeded at retrieving her head, and now she was living out of Shinra Kishitani's home.

While they would fall into mutual love eventually, at this point in time it was an entirely one-sided infatuation on Shinra's part, and Celty was still unaware of the feelings that were slowly building within her.

Even still, she felt that she had picked up some amount of knowledge about the human psyche and its foibles—but these phone calls Shinra made were still beyond her.

"What was that about?"

"Huh? I was just inviting Shizuo and Izaya to tomorrow's coming-of-age ceremony, that's all."

"Well, with the way you hung up on them, they're not going to be motivated to come, are they?"

"Oh, that's where you're wrong, Celty. Shizuo and Izaya are actually *more* likely to come when you try to push them around like that. Shizuo will want to hit me, and Orihara will want to make snide remarks," Shinra explained.

Celty thought that made sense at first, but after imagining the result, had to clarify with him. *"Wait a second, doesn't that mean that if they both show up tomorrow, they'll see each other?"*

"Yes, that's right," Shinra said simply.

Celty tilted what would have been her head in bemusement. *"It is? You're just going to…"*

"Listen, Celty. They're both twenty now. Twenty years old. It would be one thing if they were still in the throes of their teenage angst, but they're adults now. They're too old to just jump for the throat as soon as they see each other," Shinra explained, eyes sparkling. "So I think it's a good opportunity to have them make up. And aren't I so mature for being the go-between to help solve this rift?"

"I…I guess so…"

He was so confident that Celty couldn't bring herself to argue with his point. Maybe human beings really did mature after this coming-of-age ceremony happened. Did that mean that the rough-and-tumble men she saw on TV were actually *more* mature than they had been before? Maybe they had been even worse, threatening travelers with chainsaws and stealing their water and seeds.

Considering that very real possibility, Celty chose to believe in the potential of the human spirit and let Shinra do what he wanted without comment.

As it turned out, he was dead wrong.

♂♀

The next day, Tokyo Metropolitan Theatre, Ikebukuro

"And after an address from the ward mayor, we will introduce our special guest. You'll get a greeting from a current member of Toshima Ward's own Rakuei Gym, the German mixed martial arts champion visiting Japan to defend his crown, the one and only Traugott Geissendorfer."

The Metropolitan Theatre was packed with newly matured adults, and the crowd was given a lively splash of color by the feminine kimonos.

The very large and imposing guest of honor gave an address to the crowd, and the rest of the event was proceeding without incident.

"Bet I'm stronger than you!" jeered a thuggish newly matured adult around the front row. He threw an empty beer bottle at the speaker.

But a moment later, the bottle had been cut clean in two with a hand chop, and the speaker hadn't missed a syllable of his speech. The audience froze; the man who'd thrown the bottle immediately sobered up, and no one else dared heckle the guest of honor.

"Life is full of tribulations. You are free to run away from them. No one has the right to demand that you fight beyond your means and get hurt," continued the fighter, unperturbed, in perfectly fluent Japanese. "However, if you only allow yourself to be swept along by outside forces, you will eventually lose the ability to make a choice. At least ensure you have the will to determine which direction to run, and the strength to move yourself toward that escape. Even fleeing requires courage."

The speech continued quietly and without incident—until the occasional vibration and sound of destruction issued from outside the building, and what sounded like screams began to trickle into the mix.

The next moment, the doors to the auditorium flew right off their hinges, and a vending machine hurtled inside.

A mass of several hundred pounds shot toward the stage as though it had been launched by a catapult, eliciting a wave of screams from the audience that had just quieted down.

But Traugott merely snorted, collected his breath, and grabbed the hurtling machine with a spinning grab of his own style. Like magic, the vending machine's momentum stopped, and it landed with a thud on the stage.

Traugott inspected the machine, which had landed right side up, and continued his speech.

"When standing before a vending machine, a person is faced with many options. What to drink, or whether to drink at all. If the same drink option has two buttons, do you press the right one or the left? Even in seemingly meaningless choices like this, the very act of choosing necessitates igniting the soul and burning its fuel—"

Now something else flew into the room.

It was a newly made adult wearing glasses and a white lab coat.

"Aaaaah…"

Rather humorously, the figure flew toward the stage just as the vending machine had, revealing itself to be none other than Shinra Kishitani. Traugott caught him, just as he'd caught the vending machine, and sat him down next to it.

"...Huh? Wait, I'm alive?"

Shinra had pulled through perfectly unharmed, much to his own surprise. He looked around for answers, but Traugott was once again forging ahead with his speech.

"You are all going to meet many people in your adult lives. Develop the strength to deal with how they choose to live, or at least the flexibility to accept whatever they throw your way. A hard fist is only one form of human strength. Choose the form of strength that best fits you and make the most of—"

But the screams outside got even louder, so Traugott finally broke off and bowed to the audience of young adults.

"...Pardon me, but I believe I will pause the speech for just a brief recess."

He hopped down from the stage and sprinted toward the commotion outside of the theater.

The crowd was left stunned. This had to be an act of some kind.

It clearly wasn't, but many in the audience chose to prioritize their peace of mind by assuming that it was all part of the entertainment.

Of course, those from Raijin High School were all perfectly aware of who was responsible for the uproar.

"...They really freakin' did it this time," grumbled Kadota, wearing a full formal and traditional *montsuki* hakama, as Shinra scurried off of the stage. "Not that I'm particularly surprised..."

♂♀

Years earlier, on the street, Ikebukuro

"So what happened after that?" Tom asked.

Shizuo explained, "Simon happened to be in the area, so him and Traugott held me down while the fleabrain scampered off... The police were about to get involved, but somehow that Traugott guy managed to explain it as 'part of the ceremony.'"

"Ahh, I see."

"I don't think he did it to help me. I think he just wanted to avoid making Toshima look bad… Anyway, he said to me, 'Being weak is not a crime. Strengthen yourself, young man.'"

"…He called *you* weak…? I'm sure he meant mentally. That fighter's one hell of a guy. I can see why you said you look up to him," Tom said, flabbergasted.

"Yeah. I realized that I'm actually a weak person…and it feels like I just recently *finally* got a bit stronger."

"I request a correction. Sir Shizuo has been strong from the founding of Heaven and Earth. It is a pre-ordained system," Vorona spoke up from the back.

Shizuo just smirked. "If I am any stronger, it's because of you and Tom."

"?"

She just gave him a look.

Tom shrugged and rolled his eyes, choosing not to comment. He started off for the next collection point. Shizuo followed him, reminiscing on the past and muttering to himself.

"But if I ever manage to get my act together, I'd like to try that coming-of-age ceremony thing."

♂♀

Tokyo

"You know, if we'd kept going, I could have had Shizu sent to prison for good. That stupid Traugott fighter really messed things up for me," Izaya reminisced, shaking his head sadly.

His assistant, Namie, replied, "At the very least, it sounds like you never belonged anywhere near a coming-of-age ceremony."

"Are you trying to say that I'm immature?"

"You are a child and always will be. That's why you keep teasing that monster Shizuo Heiwajima. You're just like those kids who keep poking hornet's nests," she said coldly.

Izaya shrugged. "I happen to think that there's no difference between adults and children. People remain children for as long as they live, and sometimes kids are more grown-up than the actual adults. We are always incomplete, and that in turn is what completes the human being."

The usual smile was back on his face as he muttered to himself.

"It's why I love humanity."

♂♀

Kawagoe Highway, Shinra's apartment

"You know, I still remember that ceremony, even now. I literally could have died that day," Shinra said casually

Exasperated, Celty typed, *"I still regret taking you at your word and letting you go."*

"Maybe people don't change as easily as I thought. There's a Japanese saying, 'The soul of a three-year-old lasts to a hundred.' And there's another one: 'The sparrow still remembers its dance at a hundred.'"

"Do sparrows live to be a hundred?"

"That's what you have a problem with?"

At this point, Celty and Shinra's fairly typical conversation was interrupted by their uninvited visitor: Shinra's father, Shingen Kishitani.

"Young folks these days are so pathetic. The coming-of-age ceremony is only a name now. They don't have what it takes on the inside," he said, wearing his white gas mask.

Shinra made a face and replied, "I don't know, Dad, you're nearly fifty and you certainly don't, either."

"You say that to your own biological father, Shinra?! When I was twenty, I'd done all the growing I'd ever need to do!" Shingen boasted.

Celty typed, *"I see. Then I suppose your standards were just wrong from the start,"* and showed it to him.

"You say that to your own father-in-law, Celty?!"

"Also, I have difficulty even imagining you showing up to your coming-of-age ceremony."

Shingen stroked the inhaler part of his gas mask and nodded. "Indeed, when I was twenty, the ceremony was the last of my concerns…but now, the story can be told. The Twenty Great Secrets of my twenty-year-old self!"

"No, we're good," Shinra said.

Shingen ignored him, turning to the window and speaking in a slow, dramatic narration. "It was in the twentieth year of my life… As a twenty-year-old, I was a young man, and I celebrated the twenticity of that year. I was a true twentieth-century boy when I was twenty... Long live the age of twenty!"

"He's doing a voice-over monologue!"

"How many times are you going to say the word 'twenty'?"

Shingen ignored their comments again, rapt by the memories of his past.

"Yes...I was a research student in the medical college, traveling the world in search of a new elixir! From the wine of eternal life to powder that turns one into a werewolf, even the wriggling red liquid that can be found in Germany!"

"That's not what a medical research student does."

"Pay no attention to my subtle lies! You'll never be an adult this way!"

"That was supposed to be subtle?"

Shingen continued to monologue for about twenty minutes after that. Celty and Shinra played a handheld game against each other and largely ignored him.

"And thus, I completed my coming-of-age by shooting the alien at the ruins beneath the South Pole and gained the treasure of the ancient Mayans: this pure white gas mask! But at the same moment, I had an incredible epiphany! Despite the incredible poisons the ancient civilizations created, none of them are as dangerous to humanity as modern man's photochemical smog and exhaust fumes!"

He breathed heavily, panting behind the gas mask. Without taking his eyes off his game, Shinra said, "Yes, yes, very cool."

"You know, Shinra, sometimes empty words of praise can hurt more than insults! Damn you...damn you... Just you wait! I'll make up much better lies next time! I'll show you the true power of an adult!" Shingen shouted, blubbering as he rushed out of the room.

Celty watched him go somewhat sadly, and typed, *"A coming-of-age ceremony... There's an event that I'll never experience."*

"That's not true."

"Huh?"

"It's been twenty years since you lost your head and were reborn as your new self, hasn't it? Of course...it's also been twenty years since you met me," Shinra explained, grinning like a child. "I can guarantee that you're a wonderfully mature adult by now. You're more human and grown-up than any person, Celty."

"Shinra..."

She felt herself being overcome by emotion—but also felt the creeping hand of Shinra working around her shoulder.

"Now, let's celebrate by engaging in some adult-only activi—*byuhurblp!*"

A large fan made of shadow smacked him across the room. Celty shoved her PDA into his face.

"You're the one who needs to grow up!"

♂♀

"Shit, man. I'm not your personal taxi to take you to your nerd events…"

In the parking lot, Togusa grumbled behind the wheel of the van.

Kadota said, "Hey, it's not that bad, right? Only happens once every twenty years."

This earned him a retort from Karisawa. "What are you talking about, Dotachin? The twentieth anniversary is only just beginning!"

"What?" he said, lifting an eyebrow.

Yumasaki shouted, "Next year is the twentieth anniversary of the Dengeki Prize! The year of *Oki-Den*! And *Criss Cross*!"

"And the year after that is the twentieth for Dengeki PlayStation!"

"Oh, if we're doing those, then it's also the twentieth anniversary of Dengeki PC Engine…"

"And before you know it, they'll be on the thirtieth!"

As the two of them got increasingly excited, Togusa's head slumped against the wheel. He grumbled, "Are you telling me…you want to be hanging out in my van ten years from now…?"

The city still revolves to this day.

As if to celebrate equally all those who come of age within it.

Fin

INTERMISSION D

Once she had looked through the physical photo album long enough, Celty turned back to her computer files.

"Seems like my archival method lately has been video more than still photos."

Next to her photo folder was a video folder, which she was realizing had grown to a considerable size.

"Though some people say that photos bring back the memories clearer..."

"Everyone's different that way. It's like arguing over whether developed photos or digital photo are better."

"I guess that's how it works."

"And times change. From what Dad says, when photography went from black-and-white to color, some people said that the black-and-white photos brought back the memories stronger. In the end, it's the feelings you have toward what's already familiar that affects your memories," Shinra said, a rare thoughtful comment.

Celty shrugged and typed, *"It's true that times have changed."*

She opened an Internet browser on her computer, taking her to a famous video site.

"I never would have expected that a day would come where everyone in the world can share their own videos with each other."

"It feels like a new era, doesn't it? Lots of people were also surprised when blogging became a thing, and they realized you could share your journal with the entire world."

Shinra gazed at the site with great feeling. Then, before Celty could stop him, he typed "headless rider ikebukuro" in the search bar.

"Hey, what are you—"

"Why, I'm checking on the videos that other people have taken of you, of course."

"But why?!"

"Why else? Because I want to bask in the feeling of superiority and reassurance that *I'm* the one who captures you best on video," he declared.

Celty pushed his shoulder. *"Stop this! It's embarrassing!"*

"Oh, don't be shy. Ooh, let's see what the video with the most views is... Ahh, this one..."

His face darkened, which Celty did not fail to miss. She could already guess which video it was.

"Ah...that was the one when Karisawa's group got to me..."

SIDE STORY 7: NICOCOCO!! (NICONICO NOVEL SHORT-TERM SERIAL)

SIDE STORY 7
NICOCOCO!!
(*NICONICO NOVEL* SHORT-TERM SERIAL)

[Start]
This is a twisted tale.
A tale of twisted comments.

"Let's take that video!"
"Gotta shoot for number one in the daily rankings!"
Walker Yumasaki and Erika Karisawa were equipped with a video camera and a laptop computer. If this were their usual banter toward Kadota and Togusa, they might have been ignored like usual. However…

"…Huh?"

Celty Sturluson was absolutely baffled by the unannounced visitors to her apartment building, tilting her head in confusion.
Or to be more precise, tilting the helmet that rested atop her body. Because, you see—she had no head at all.

♂♀

Celty Sturluson was not human.
She was a type of fairy commonly known as a dullahan, found from Scotland to Ireland—a being that visits the homes of those close to death to inform them of their impending end.

The dullahan carried its own severed head under its arm, rode on a two-wheeled carriage called a Cóiste Bodhar pulled by a headless horse, and approached the homes of the soon-to-die. Anyone foolish enough to open the door was drenched with a basin full of blood. Thus the dullahan, like the banshee, made its name as a herald of ill fortune in European folklore.

But that was all in the past.
Now she lived a life of love and happiness with a man named Shinra Kishitani, both as a living urban legend and as a woman.

It was this peaceful life that was broken by their sudden arrival.
"What kind of video…?"
"Oh, come on. If you're in Japan and you're talking about making a video, it's gotta be for Niconico! Nico Video!" Karisawa stated.

Yumasaki beamed, the kind of smile that Niconico was named after. "That's right! In fact, Karisawa was a regular user since back when it was Niconico Beta!"

"Uh, well…I'm aware of Niconico, but… Huh? If you knew it when it was in beta, then how old are you…?"

"All right, I think we've covered the boring details well enough by now!" Karisawa said, clapping her hands to bring the topic to a close. "So, what kinda video do you want to make, Celcchi? Wanna try commentary over a free game that's okay to stream without any copyright shenanigans?"

"No, I think I might be the wrong person to ask…about commentary."

"You'll be fine; there's text-to-speech software for that. Or if need be, you can just do a no-commentary playthrough. The only thing that matters is that the video is entertaining."

"Hang on. Why are you doing a video, again? And why come to me?" Celty asked, quite naturally.

Karisawa shook her head sadly. "Aw, darn, I was hoping you wouldn't notice… You're too smart, Celcchi."

"Notice what…?"

"Well, uh… Ya know? It's my own personal issue, so I feel really bad bringing it up to you like this, but…," Karisawa murmured, trailing off, so Yumasaki picked up the slack.

"The thing is, Karisawa has a rival on Niconico."

"A rival?"

"Check out this video first."

"W-wait, Yumacchi, stop! I can't handle her watching it in front of me!" Karisawa begged, but Yumasaki ignored her and connected his laptop into a wireless router so that he could load a particular page on Nico Video.

The video was titled "I Tried Singing Opera in Cosplay @ Eternal de Charmonte," and it featured Karisawa dressed up as some anime character, singing opera with a mask covering the top half of her face.

"No! Stop! Don't listen to it!" Karisawa pleaded, struggling to stop him. Yumasaki put her into a pinion hold, so Celty focused on the sound of Karisawa's singing on the laptop.

Though she had no ears, the shadow that surrounded her being could pick out the sound of the voice clearer than any human ear could. Overcome with emotion, she pointed her smartphone screen at Karisawa.

"You…you never told me…you were so good at singing!"

"I know, isn't it something? Among all my anime-song friends, Karisawa's practically a legend."

"Auuugh, it's not true. I'm so embarraaaassed…"

Her face was completely red now, and her eyes swam and roved. It was almost impossible to imagine her acting this way, based on her usual demeanor.

"Anyway…is this 'Eternal de Charmonte' your stage name or something…?"

"Oh, yeah! That's right! Isn't it cool?!" she replied, suddenly all sparkling.

Celty felt a cold sweat break out on the inside. *"I see… So you're not embarrassed about that part of it…"*

It was another new fact for Celty to consider about the other woman.

Yumasaki continued, "So, this Charmonte in the video has a rival named Blizzard La Blizzardia. She's really good at singing and does cosplay, so it's a natural comparison…"

"And?"

"One day, they were on a Skype chat together, and the competitive hackles rose, until the other girl said, 'I know ***, the famous game streamer. You don't seem like you have any friends, though,' and Karisawa snapped back, 'I have lots of really famous and amazing friends!'"

"*…And?*" Celty prompted. She still couldn't see where this was going.

"They went back and forth a little more and decided to have each friend upload their video to Niconico, so they could compete and see who got more views and bookmarks and smiles, from what I understand!"

"*I see, yes. Compared to the opera singing from a moment ago, this turned out to have a much stupider reasoning behind it.*"

After a pause, Celty increased the font size on her smartphone so that she could try shouting.

"*You absolute idiot!*"

The text flew fast and furious from her fingers. When she was done, she thrust the message toward Karisawa and Yumasaki.

"*Why would you compete using a video?! Are you NPCs in a mahjong game that tell the hero that you have to fight using mahjong?! Are your brains on video?! Is this what younger kids do nowadays when they need to rebel?! Are you the kind of people who illegally upload DVD special features, then claim innocence because it's for 'promotional purposes'?!*"

Her shoulders heaved up and down with exertion, then she resumed typing with great ferocity.

"*Obviously, each of your followers is going to pretend to be one of the other and post insults and trash the other one, or try to pad the comments on your video until you get found out and raked over the coals, or try to buy big view counts! This is all wrong! Niconico is called that because it's supposed to make everyone smile!*"

"Well, I can reassure you that I'm a mature adult, so that won't happen with me."

"*Mature adults don't torture hooligans in their friends' vans!*"

"Let's just set that aside for now… I came to ask you for help because I thought you might be able to make some truly exciting videos. I'm just asking your opinion. It won't be a hassle," Karisawa promised, ignoring the more salacious details that Celty was pointing out. Oddly, this helped Celty calm down a bit.

"*I didn't want to say this, but the motorcycle officers have their eye on me, so if the video ends up with revealing information in the background, and someone figures out my address, and it causes the word to go out on social media that 'the Headless Rider got arrested because she posted a video of herself online,' I would never live it down.*"

"Well, that's probably your own fault for catching their eye. You'll just have to live with the consequences."

"Yeah, that's true. You're the one committing the most criminal acts, Celcchi."

"Y-you know, when you put it that way, I feel terrible about it..."

Now that they had her over a barrel, Celty realized she would just have to play along...

"I've heard your tale of woe," said the owner of the apartment, Shinra Kishitani, as he opened a nearby door. "You leave me no choice. In order to help you prove that your friend Celty is truly amazing, I am willing to help."

"Do you know how to make videos, Shinra?"

It better not turn out to be something like, "I Tried Surgery: A Black-Market Doctor Attempts to Heal Himself," or whatever, Celty thought nervously.

Shinra beamed and said, "I'll release a portion of the hidden videos I've been taking of you for the past ten years! I can't do all of them, because I'm greedy and want to keep you to myself...but knowing your charms, Celty, I'm sure it'll break a million views in no time!"

A few minutes later, Shinra had been trussed up with Celty's shadow weapon and left to dangle, while she typed out a message to Karisawa and Yumasaki with obvious exhaustion.

"All right... I'll give you as much help as I can, as long as you forget what Shinra just said."

Hours later

Of course, having said that, she thought, setting up her laptop after Karisawa had left, *what am I actually able to help out with when it comes to making a video?*

She looked at her homepage on Nico Video.

She had registered under the username Setton. Celty started out by watching the lone video she'd uploaded in the past.

The video's title was "[Beautiful Stuff] Rooftops with Great Views, twelve in all! [Rooftop videos]"

She had recorded footage from the roofs of buildings she liked and edited them together.

I haven't seen this in a few years...but with the way I named my video, I don't think I can make fun of Karisawa's handle name, either. What if they're all bashing my clip and saying it's really boring?

Nervous, she checked the stats on the video.

Views: 12 Comments: 0 Bookmarks: 2

Oh...ohhhhh...

"Whatcha watching, Celty?" said a voice, causing her to flinch.

Shinra came and looked over her shoulder at the video on the screen.

"Wow, Celty, I didn't know you uploaded a video! You could have told me. I'd have spent fifty thousand yen on turning it into an ad!" he exclaimed. When he took a closer look, his eyes lit up. "Wow! The comments section is packed!"

He was looking at the great volumes of comments that, in typical Niconico fashion, were displayed scrolling over the screen from right to left, and saying things like "It's so beautiful," "Perfect scenery," and "I love being on the roof."

"Really? Well, it's nothing special, anyway," Celty said, trembling slightly.

Shinra grinned and said, "Well, Celty, this is rather strange. Can you tell me why every single person is commenting using black text, rather than the default white?"

"I...don't know."

"Also, there's something about these black text comments that looks different from the black text I'm used to seeing..."

"Must be your mind playing tricks on you."

If Celty were human, she would be drowning in nervous sweat by this point. Shinra could see right through her story, and his grin got even wider.

"Listen, Celty, even if you were, say, creating shadow letters and running them across the screen to fool me, I would still love you," he said, tenderly consoling his frozen partner. "That oddly small-minded part of you is just one of the many reasons I'm so fond of you."

Celty scrunched up the black text scrolling across the computer screen and thrust her smartphone into Shinra's face.

"Don't react like that! It's only making me feel more pathetic!"

* * *

This was how Celty got embroiled in Karisawa's video rivalry.

With the Dollars gone, and Ikebukuro taking on a different color in their absence, a new story was unfolding.

A low-stakes tale of the Headless Rider as an urban legend completely entrenched in the foibles of the modern world.

♂♀

[Expand]

Days later, Kawagoe Highway, apartment building

Celty Sturluson, Ikebukuro's Headless Rider, was in a panic.

Her friend Karisawa had asked her to do the impossible—upload a video and get onto the daily ranking—and she had shortsightedly agreed.

While there was still time before the deadline, Celty's previous attempt at making a video was a catastrophe with twelve views and no comments, and she couldn't begin to guess what to go for next.

Hmm… Maybe I should watch some popular videos and take notes.

She decided that it would be best to see what worked for others, so she opened her laptop and started viewing the most popular spots in the Niconico rankings.

Number one on the list is…a game commentary video. Yumasaki and Karisawa were talking about that, too…but I'm unable to do vocal commentary. Plus there are issues with distribution rights, and I don't know the difference between a game that's cool to upload and one that's going to get me in trouble. Plus, now there are games that the companies are okay with people uploading videos of, as long as they abide by certain conditions… Ugh, this is giving me a headache.

Realizing that she was already hitting a stumbling block before she even got to the issue of a video's popularity, Celty felt more aware than ever that she was in over her (absent) head.

I guess I'll start with a free game. What's popular in the horror sphere…? Blue Kappa. Hmm, let's go with this one.

She found a horror game that had been in and out of the rankings for the past few years and downloaded it.

I hear it's super scary, but I'm not bothered by ghosts and youkai and things like that. Heh-heh-heh. Kappa are actually kinda cute.

Excited by the thought of playing the game and blasting through scenes that would have other players trembling in terror, Celty started up the program.

♂♀

One hour later

"Celty? Celty, your favorite show is coming on!" called out Shinra Kishitani, the Headless Rider's live-in partner, popping into the room.

But she was nowhere to be found.

"Huh? That's weird. Where could Celty be?"

He glanced around the room curiously—then strode right up to the closet and pulled the door open.

"Heeeere's *Celty*!"

An enormous fish about three feet in size, made of pure shadow, thrust itself forward and clobbered Shinra.

"Ogopogo!"

He rolled across the room until he came to a stop, then saw Celty crouching and shivering in the closet, vibrating like a phone notification.

"…Celty?" he said, still sprawled out on the floor. She finally turned toward him and hesitantly emerged from the closet. Once she was certain that no suspicious shadows were around, she hurried over to Shinra and shoved her smartphone in his face.

"S-sorry, Shinra! Are you all right?!"

"Of course I'm all right!" he said, immediately bouncing up and giving her an energetic thumbs-up. "I would be fine, no matter what kind of unfair and one-sided violence you committed against me! The entire world could revile you as a needlessly crude and abusive heroine, but I would and *will* always be on your side! I won't let anyone else have you, and if I have to become a masochist for you, I'll do it! Now step on me! Do Hindu squats on my stomach!"

"*All right, all right, I'm sorry. Just calm down,*" Celty said, trying to get Shinra to stop rolling around on the ground with his cheeks flushed with excitement. She checked around for anything amiss.

"So what's the matter, Celty? Why were you hiding in the closet?"

"I-it was the game."

"What game?" He glanced at the desk, where a game was currently on the screen of the computer there. "What is this?"

"It's a g-g-game called Blue Kappa, *and I assumed it would be like the kind where you run around a mansion trying to escape from the kappa,*" she explained, hiding behind Shinra's back, "*but the blue kappa wasn't a youkai at all; it was an alien, and every day a few more of the townsfolk get abducted and taken over by the aliens! And at the end, the entire town itself turns into an alien...and the walls and floor are blue kappa alien faces! Aieeeee!*"

"...Is it an adventure game? Or a visual novel?"

"*No, it's a farming sim.*"

"Oh, that's horrifying. Who comes up with that crap?" Shinra remarked, feeling fear for a different reason. He shut down the game that had terrified Celty so badly. "There, you're safe now. There are no aliens."

"R-really?"

"Really. None. Nobody's here. Nobody's here. Nobody's here... *Peekaboo!*" he shouted, launching himself toward Celty—but she had seen it coming. She easily avoided his lunge and slammed him into the closet.

"Oooh, ouch... Anyway, you *really* don't like aliens, do you?"

"*It's outer space! When the Grand Cross happens and all the planets of the solar system are arranged in a straight line, it means a black hole will be photon-belted right into our midst!*"

"Celty, calm down. First of all, it is categorically impossible for a Grand Cross to coincide with all the planets lining up."

"*O-oh...*"

At last, Celty seemed to be regaining her nerve. She stopped trembling and put her arm around Shinra's shoulder.

"*Thank you, Shinra. I don't think I'm cut out for commentating on horror games.*"

"Ahh, this is for Yumasaki and Karisawa's thing?" Shinra said, realizing at once that it was about the Niconico video upload. He beamed at Celty. "Well, if you really like games, maybe you should move away from horror and try beating a really, really hard game instead."

"*A hard game...? Like the kind where you die over and over, memorizing the layout and growing ever more paranoid that everything is a trap?*"

"Yes, exactly. Of course, you're not going to make a splash by playing a famous, well-known game at this point. You'll need to play some super-hard obscure game that no one's heard of."

"*That no one's heard of? Are you sure one even exists?*" Celty wondered, tilting her helmet.

But Shinra had just the person in mind.

"Yeah. It's a game that Orihara made. I guarantee the difficulty is legit."

♂♀

Back in high school

"What are you doing?" Shinra asked curiously.

His classmate, Izaya Orihara, had a laptop open on his desk. "I'm just killing time. Making a little video game on my own."

"Video game?"

The boy wore a full black *gakuran* uniform, but his smile was even darker than the fabric as he handed Shinra a CD-ROM.

"Here's a copy of it, if you want to try."

"Are you sure? What kind of game is it?"

"It's meant to test the limits of human perseverance. It's not that good, though, so I'm not planning to put it up online."

♂♀

Present day, Shinra's apartment

"Oooh, hey, it still runs on the latest OS," Shinra murmured happily. Celty, however, felt anxious.

"*Is this safe? I don't trust a game he created…*"

"Yeah, totally fine. There were no viruses when I ran it."

"*Oh, so you played it before,*" Celty commented.

He smiled breezily and nodded. "Yeah. And I stopped playing after ten seconds."

"*What the heck? I have no idea how bad this game is supposed to be, but ten seconds seems too short,*" she said, paying attention to the start screen.

* * *

Bedeviled! Izaya's Castle! Or, Izaya's Challenge

"I take that back, Shinra. I'm already irritated," she said, having felt so strongly that moments after seeing the title screen, she had already created a text file and typed her annoyance into it.

"I know. The more you know Orihara, the more obnoxious it feels. And I'm sure that he wouldn't have given this game to anyone who didn't know him very well."

"He's the worst."

"It's just our luck that Shizuo didn't have a computer of his own. If he'd played this, he might have destroyed every single computer within a three-mile radius."

The thought of her wild bartender-vest-wearing acquaintance made Celty's spine freeze. But for now, she started the game.

After clicking the start button, a man appeared on screen who seemed to be the player character. The arrow keys moved him left and right, while the space bar made him jump.

All right. Seems like an orthodox action game.

"Or so you'd think, right?"

"Stop reading my mind, it's creepy."

But whatever. It's a game made by Izaya, so I can already guess how it goes. There's probably a really hard quick time event or something in the middle, or it turns into a racing game, then a mahjong game, then an RPG, then a deductive adventure game—all these detours and sidetracks meant to annoy the player, right? As long as I know what I'm getting into, there's nothing to be afraid of.

But as soon as she started to move the character…

Oops, already with the pits, huh?

A hole opened at the bottom of the screen, and her character fell through it.

But it was not a game over. The background turned black, but the character continued to fall, onward and onward at the center of the screen, leaving a visual trail that went upward.

Ah. So it goes to a different screen. I wonder if there's another path at the bottom of the earth?

…

………

................*How long is he going to fall?!*

After about thirty seconds of this, the screen changed.

Beside the falling character, text began to rise from the bottom of the screen, moving very slowly.

The character you control is falling perpetually into a dark hole. He is not greeted by the shock and pain of impact, but is subjected to the fear of his ever-lengthening plummet. In time, the fear turns to uncertainty. Will there even be an end? Has he been trapped in a cycle of endless descent with no conclusion, fated to fall forever? Eventually, the uncertainty turns to loss. The fear and anxiety will be leached from his heart, and he will feel as though he is losing even his past experiences and emotions. Then again, maybe he has a different thought. Did he ever have those emotions in the first place? His life was over the moment he fell into the hole. Has he left all of his memories and feelings and reasons for existence up on the surface, in the light? So who is he? Eventually, even the concept of an attempt to derive the meaning of his existence as he falls will fade away, and he will wonder why he was even born, allowed as he is to do nothing but fall. His character will become a pitiable symbol of falling itself. If there's any emotion he's left with, it's hatred toward you, the player. Why did you have me carelessly walk forward? You knew this game was made by Izaya Orihara, so why were you so deluded as to believe that the floor before you was what it appeared? This is your fault. I've lost everything and become nothing but a program that falls endlessly, and it's all your fault. I hate you I hate you I hate you I hate you I hate you I hate you I hate you I hate you... I'm sure that's what he's thinking. But you need not feel guilty. You're just the same. That's right, this character that expresses falling with nothing more than a mild vertical afterimage effect is depicting the life of you, the player. How many seconds, how many hours have you spent on this game? Have you discovered anything in this meaningless game that might actually enrich your life somehow? What are games for? Killing boredom? Does your boredom lie dead at your feet? Or have you merely enhanced it with further tribulations, increasing the minutes you've wasted of your life? And if there's no way to alleviate the boredom than through pain, what makes you any different from this falling character—

The text continued, seemingly endless, at a painful pace of one line every five seconds or so, rising up the length of the screen.

At first, Celty patiently read each word of it, but eventually her endurance gave way, and she asked Shinra, *"Hey...it's not responding to any controls."*

"It was the same for me. I fell into the hole after ten seconds, and there was no way to keep playing after that."

"So how long does this obnoxiously edgelordy text keep going?"

"I just let it keep running for an hour, and it was still going. Sometimes you just really have to hand it to Izaya's restless energy."

Celty had had enough. She clicked the X button at the top right corner of the window.

What's this? Giving up already? Running away won't solve your problems. But if you truly want to avert your eyes from reality, you can just open up Task Manager and end the entire process, can't you? You'll just know deep down that you admitted defeat and let me win.

The pop-up window had appeared instead of shutting down the program, and Celty barely held back the urge to smash the computer screen.

"Arrrgh! What the hell is this?!"

"Right? It's hard, isn't it? Hard to stay motivated to beat it, at least."

"That's not the kind of difficulty I'm looking for!"

"Yeah, but you had a feeling this was coming, didn't you?" said Shinra, trying to dissuade Celty from flying into a violent rage. "Speaking of which, there was one person named Tsukumoya who actually managed to get to the end and send his thoughts about the game... Izaya was creeped out. I told him I didn't know who it was or remember giving them the game in the first place."

"Whoa, freaky. He isn't an alien...is he?" She started to feel another chill run down her back and quickly changed the topic to dispel it. *"First of all, how I even do commentary for something like this?"*

"Well, guess what? You don't have to! I've already filmed your reactions of anguish and barely suppressed rage, so the heavy lifting's already been done!" Shinra said, his expression blissful. He gave her a thumbs-up; in his other hand was a high-definition camera. "Once I upload this to Nico Video, *everyone* will be smiling over your charms, Celty!"

"......"

Minutes later, having trussed up Shinra and left him in the corner of the room, Celty proceeded to consider what to put up on Niconico.

Hmmm. I don't think game commentary is going to work out for me. There's got to be some video that will serve as inspiration...

She stared at the screen until something occurred to her.

Oops, I nearly forgot. My Niconico points are nearly about to expire. I've still got 2,800 points left, so I need to use them up...

Considering this a good opportunity, she decided to use the online currency she'd stocked up to watch a movie and improve her mood.

Let's see... I'll watch a ghost movie, perhaps. Oh, hey, Dark Skies *is on Niconico Channel right now. I was always curious about that one after I saw a poster of it on Sixtieth Floor Street. Apparently it was made by some of the people who did* Paranormal Activity...*and I'm fine watching ghost movies. This should be fun. Though* Dreamcatcher *is pretty tempting, too. That one looks horror-ish. I'm also curious about* The Fourth Kind.

So, which one do I watch...?

Two hours later, having finished her selection, Celty was back in the closet, shivering and trembling for all she was worth.

What had she seen in the movie that made her react like this?

The answers can be found...on Nico Video.

"...Umm, Celty? You can undo your shadow ropes now. Celty? ... Celty?"

♂♀

[Twist]

Days later, Ikebukuro shopping district

Ikebukuro was the same as always on this day.

Shortly after seven in the evening, the crowds passing one another on the street included office workers on the way home, students enjoying a very long after-school period, and various people whose appearances didn't immediately connect to a particular living.

Emotions of all types were etched into the faces of those who walked the streets, from bright laughter to exhausted sighing after work, all mingling into the atmosphere of a city that remained as lively as it ever was.

Except for one thing.

A suspicious-looking shadow astride a pitch-black motorcycle with no headlight and no license plate—the Headless Rider, wandering around with a camcorder in her hands.

"Hey, it's Celty. What are you doing?"

The Headless Rider, Celty Sturluson, had been watching the city from the shadows until she was called over by a longtime friend, Shizuo Heiwajima.

With his bartender's vest, he was a fairly visible person on the streets, but not nearly as much as Celty was. He had finished his work shift and was on the way home when he spotted Celty skulking around behind a utility pole and called out to her.

"Oh…Sh-Shizuo. It's been a while."

"Yo. What's with the video camera? You doing a job?"

"No…it's more like a hobby… I was wondering if I could capture some interesting footage, or maybe something weird and paranormal…"

"Paranormal?"

Given that Celty herself was a paranormal phenomenon, it was a strange thing to hear her say.

"Um, basically, I'm trying to take a video that I can upload to Nico Video, but I haven't found many good opportunities."

"What the hell is Nico Video?"

"…Umm…I guess you'd call it an online service that allows you to upload your own videos so that everyone else can comment on them and share them…"

She kept the explanation as simple as possible, since Shizuo didn't know much about the Internet. It would've been pointless to go into greater detail, and her anticipation was accurate.

"Ah…it's an Internet thing," he said, disappointed, and scratched his cheek with a finger. "I don't think I'm any good at that online stuff. If you get mad, you can't just reach out and punch the other person, so I'd just end up destroying all my own stuff instead."

"…That's true. You're probably better off not checking it out, Shizuo."

Plus, he's got absolutely zero ability to avoid and ignore trolling, she thought but prudently did not say. At this point, she figured she could just tell him what she was doing.

"At any rate, I'm trying to take a video that's entertaining and will draw everyone's interest. Sometimes I spot people doing strange things or doing some kind of street performance, but I can't just film them without permission... What I'd really like to do is capture a freak occurrence. Like a dance between a pink elephant and white crocodile that escaped from the circus. Heh-heh-heh-heh-heh-heh."

"Uh, you think you might be losing it a little?"

"M-maybe I am."

"First of all, you don't just *happen* to capture rare events on film just by standing around," Shizuo explained, taking a sip from the can in his hand.

"Yeah, I know that, but..."

While Celty continued to watch the environs around her with camera in hand, Shizuo finished his drink and began to fold the metal can with his fingers. "It's best when nothing happens," he said. "Take a video of the city at peace. Then you can watch it and relax. That's the best thing of all."

As he said this, he used only the strength of his fingertips to carefully stretch out the metal can.

"Well, if it makes people smile, that would be best of all, of course... So I guess it can be a peaceful video too, huh? Maybe if I got a video of someone with a really incredible skill that no one else can imitate..."

"A skill, huh?" Shizuo repeated, transforming the can in his hands. Even the thicker, heavier base of the can was like putty to him, easily folded without much resistance. "In that case, you can't just hang around like this, huh? Not that I'm the best guy to give advice, but maybe you should take out your camera with a clear purpose in mind."

Ultimately, his monstrous strength compacted the metal can until it had been compressed into a cube the size of a die. Not even a vise could have accomplished this; the material was so dense that it seemed the folded metal surfaces were pressed permanently together.

"Well, that's true...and I doubt that I'm going to just find some person with a unique skill like that."

"Probably true. I don't know why you want to take this video, but good luck with it," Shizuo said, tossing the cube into the nearby bin specifically for cans. He turned toward his home with the clattering of metal behind him.

Shizuo's right. If it were that easy to come across something truly remarkable, everyone would be doing it all the time, Celty lamented. She put away the camera and headed for the motorcycle she'd parked nearby.

She seemed entirely unaware of the rather remarkable and inhuman feat that a man had just achieved, now resting inside the trash can just steps away.

♂♀

"Oh! It's the Headless Rider! Heya!"

"……"

Minutes later, while cruising through the city, Celty happened across a pair of familiar twins. It was the one with glasses who called out to her.

"Oh, uh… Izaya's sisters…"

"I'm Mairu! And this is Kuru!"

"……"

In contrast to Mairu Orihara, the lively younger twin, the older one, Kururi Orihara, silently bowed her head.

"So what's up? Whatcha doin'? Work?"

"Uh, not exactly… Oh, but this is good timing." Celty had always had a connection of sorts to these sisters, and given how desperate she was for help, decided to ask for their advice. *"This might seem like a strange question, but…do you know what Nico Video is?"*

"Yeah, we do!"

"Could you tell me what kind of videos you like to watch on there?"

They were students in high school. Celty didn't know what percentage of Niconico viewers were teen girls, but she figured that learning the tastes of young folks would be helpful to her quest. However…

"The dirty ones!"

"…Huh?"

"The ones where girls are going *guhee-hee, guhee-hee* and dancing half-naked!"

"I've never heard someone use the phrase 'guhee-hee, guhee-hee' before…" Celty replied, unsure of how to react to it.

Mairu continued, "You know that Kuru and I uploaded a video once? We were dancing together."

"Oh, interesting."

They were pretty to look at, and the novelty of them being twins would surely get them lots of views if the dancing was good. Celty was going to ask how many plays their video got, but Mairu beat her to the punch.

"Unfortunately, they deleted it."

"*Huh?*"

"They said it violated the part of the guidelines about how 'Sexual, obscene, or violent acts, as well as anything designed to be extremely unpleasant, are prohibited'…"

"*You're teenage girls; you shouldn't be taking videos that violate the guidelines! In fact, nobody should be doing that!*" Celty typed, flustered, much to Mairu's delight.

"Nah, it's fine. We didn't get in trouble with the police…but it was a close one."

"*Nothing about this sounds fine!*"

"It really was fine. We weren't naked or anything. It was mostly Kuru's fault for moving too sexily. As we were dancing, I was getting so turned on that I started drooling."

"*Fine, whatever. Sorry I asked. I really don't want to know anything more about this.*"

One thing you can say about them: they are definitely Izaya's sisters, Celty thought, resuming her ride through the streets. *But maybe that's just the kind of standards kids these days have? I don't really know any regular young people. They don't even need to be young, though—I just want to know how ordinary people think. I'll go around and ask for more opinions.*

♂♀

Russia Sushi

"A video? Perfect, you can shoot a promo video for our restaurant," said Denis, the owner of Russia Sushi.

Celty said nothing, feeling a sudden chill run down her spine.

Simon showed up with a sushi platter and began to dance with it in front of her camera. "Hey! Sushi good! Very healthy, fill your stomach, fill your dreams. Eel, tuna, crab, urchin, roe, shad and perch and seared salmon. Eat sushi, good for you. More you eat, thinner you get: sushi diet. Eat sushi and get girls. You win lottery, win new job, travel to paradise. Russia Sushi is good sushi, number-one hit in America," he said.

While she caught Simon's truly nonsensical sales pitch and dance on camera, Celty sadly turned to the owner and showed him her smartphone screen.

"Actually…you're not allowed to advertise a product or service on Niconico without the company's approval."

Denis sharpened his knife and briefly glanced up at Celty.

"I see… Well, you'll just have to get that permission for us, then."

"Don't ask the impossible!"

♂♀

Back door, Russia Sushi

Just after she had said goodbye to Denis and Simon, Celty spotted an acquaintance who had come around the back of the restaurant to deliver crab, so she decided to ask him for his opinion.

"Nico Video, eh? Yeah, I'm aware of it."

His name was Akabayashi.

He was a lieutenant of the Awakusu-kai, a yakuza group that controlled part of Ikebukuro. In short, he was someone with a lot of weight in the underworld behind the scenes.

"For reasons I won't go into, I need to upload a video that will garner a lot of attention…and I don't know what kind of video to make…"

"Ah, I see. Well, if you don't mind using one of mine, I got some videos that might be a hit with the right audience."

"You do?!" Celty exclaimed, latching on to this surprise revelation.

"Yup. Secret videos that haven't been made public in any way. You'll only find 'em on my phone."

"What kind of videos are they…?"

"…Once you've heard, you can't unhear it."

"Huh?" She suddenly felt a bit unnerved.

Akabayashi continued in hushed tones, "This is the kind of video that we deal in. If you wanna take it public, you gotta be ready to fight for your life."

"What does that mean…?"

"There are many kinds of videos out there. Let's say that there are freaks who really wanna see the moment that people die. Once they find out there's money in that, some folks are gonna start makin' those videos just for business reasons. I'm talkin' two-hour videos, no fakes, no cuts, all deaths."

Celty froze, so he went on.

"If you're asking someone in my position if I have any interesting videos…it means you wanna see videos that you don't see by the light of day…and if you wanna upload it to Niconico, it means you wanna mix the light and dark side of the world just a bit…even at the risk of your life… Do I take that as your intention?"

"S-sorry, I just remembered something else I need to do!"

"Maybe I went a little too hard on the intimidation," Akabayashi muttered to himself after Celty scampered off.

He played a video on his phone. "Of course, this is just a video of a celebrity who tried to get a little too rough with one of the girls at a place in our territory, so we beat him down, stripped him naked, and forced him to grovel. Nothing more than that."

♂♀

Ikebukuro

"Um…videos?"

Celty had been fearfully hurrying home when she happened to spot Anri Sonohara on her way home from school, and called out to the girl.

"I've never filmed anything like that… Oh, but I do have just one."

"*Really?*"

"Yes, it's a video of a really cute cat… Mika took a video of the one you had at your apartment a while back, and she sent it to my phone."

Anri pulled out her phone and started up the video to show it off. Although it was on a tiny flip-phone screen size, the video did indeed show a very adorable kitten with folded ears.

"*Oooh, that's it! That's what I've been looking for!*"

If push came to shove, couldn't she just ask to borrow this video and upload it instead? Celty was starting to feel desperate, and she was willing to beg others for help to succeed at her task.

But as the video went on, she decided against this idea. The camera eventually pulled back, revealing more of where the kitten was playing.

What she had initially thought was a rounded cushion was actually the top of Anri's body. The kitten was balancing carefully to not fall down the rather impressive slope, which was obvious even through the thick uniform jacket. The frolicking was having an effect on her chest as well.

"Ah, yes...thank you. This has been very helpful," Celty said, returning the phone and continuing on her way.

♂♀

That one's going to attract more than just cat fans, Celty thought as she rode away. *And after what I just told Izaya's sisters... Plus, I don't want to expose Anri to harm like that.*

She reflected on what had happened today.

Ultimately, nothing really helped, aside from Shizuo's encouragement... So I think I know my plan now. I'm going to make a video that only I can make!

She turned on the camcorder and used her shadow to affix it to the front of the bike, where her headlight would have gone if she had one. The engine produced a sound like a horse growling; Celty stroked the seat of the motorcycle to calm it.

Just put up with it for now, Shooter. It'll only last a little bit. Honestly, I have to say that this is a pretty great idea. At first, it'll just look like your standard motorcycle-mounted video...but along the way, I'll create a road out of shadow and start riding through the air.

Creating a path to ride on out of her own shadow to travel through the air was a truly brazen and wild feat, but Celty had done this before on multiple occasions.

This is gonna be so mysterious. I'll just make sure to put a couple effects on it to keep it vague and upload it as "special effects video flying through the Ikebukuro night sky," and it'll be perfect!

Heh-heh-heh... How should I tag it? Since I'll be pretending to do some special effects, I could put it under the "Niconico Tech Club" category... Or maybe "mystery tech." And for the affiliate ads on the side, I'll pick out a Peter Pan *storybook or something.*

It's perfect. The perfect plan!

Counting quite a few chickens before they hatched, Celty hopped onto her bike, feeling supremely confident.

"Yo," said a familiar voice, very close by.

......

A bone-freezing chill ran down her back. She turned, very slowly, in the direction of the voice.

"What are you doing, attaching a camera to that bike? Did you get a side job filming street traffic?"

In contrast to Celty's black, this large motorcycle was white.

And naturally, sitting atop the seat was a patrol officer.

Officer Kinnosuke Kuzuhara of the Metropolitan Police Department, Traffic Bureau, Mobile Division.

Rigid with terror, Celty awkwardly extended a bit of shadow to press the light switch on the camcorder. Then she reached out and showed her smartphone to the patrol officer, her mortal nemesis.

"...It's my headlight."

"......"

"......"

In her mind, Celty put on the most genial and friendly smile she possibly could.

"...You're not gonna stick to that story, are you?"

"...No."

And then the black motorcycle took off, quick as a rabbit.

♂♀

Shinra's apartment

"Wow, this is a great video. It's really intense," marveled Shinra Kishitani, watching the camcorder footage on the TV.

The imagery of Ikebukuro's streets was flying past at incredible speed from the perspective of the motorcycle, which was fleeing wildly from the pack of white police motorcycles.

"The problem is that you can't tell what's what, and you start to feel sick after a little while. I don't think people are going to want to bookmark this one, no matter how many effects you put on it to fix it up."

"I've had enough... I can't take any more of this city..."

Celty was thoroughly spent after two hours of frantic escape. She was sprawled out front-down on the sofa, reaching up to type into her smartphone.

"And the main issue is...I don't actually feel like smiling when I watch that video..."

So Celty's brilliant plan promptly fell apart, and her video had to be put on ice.

But she did not yet know that a part of her escape had actually been filmed by a friend of Karisawa's rival, Blizzard La Blizzardia, and had already been uploaded to Nico Video.

It had the simple title of "Headless Rider vs. Traffic Cops," and it was already at number seven on the overall rankings of the site.

Celty would eventually learn that she had accidentally gift-wrapped her foe a present, and the revelation would take all the wind out of her sails…

But not for a few more hours.

♂♀

[End]

Through a strange set of circumstances, the freak of Ikebukuro, Celty Sturluson, was involved in a "friendly battle" between Karisawa and her rival.

A friend of Karisawa's foe, Blizzard La Blizzardia, had captured footage of Celty fleeing from patrol officers, and managed to make it high into the video popularity rankings.

Now that she had put herself at a huge disadvantage, Celty had to wonder if there was anything she could do to salvage the situation—and at this point in time, she had no idea what the answer was.

Kawagoe Highway, Shinra's apartment

"I'm hooome," said Shinra, returning to the apartment late after a day of working as a black-market doctor, only to find the place filled with a gloomy, oppressive air. "Whoa! What's this? What happened?!"

And it wasn't just the mood.

As a matter of fact, Celty had spread her shadow all throughout the room like smoke, cutting down on the fluorescent lights and darkening the whole apartment.

"*Oh…w-welcome back, Shinra.*"

She came weaving her way through the darkness and wobbled forth to greet him.

"What's the matter, Celty?! Are you feeling unwell?!" Shinra exclaimed, rushing over.

Her fingers ran weakly over the smartphone screen.

"Uh...*I may have painted myself into a corner over this video thing...*"

Shinra did his best to calm her down and hear out her story. From what he could tell, a video showing her escape from the patrol officers had been captured and uploaded onto Nico Video, then shared widely across social media. The views and bookmarks were still climbing rapidly.

"*Sniff... Now I just feel horrible about what Karisawa might say to me if I don't win... I think I've really gone and done it now...*"

"What did you do?"

"*I...I went ahead and took this video...*"

"?"

Celty handed him a camcorder. He connected it to the computer and started up the video file.

Immediately, he was confronted with something bizarre. It was set in a darkened park after sundown with the light of the Sunshine Building in the distance, suggesting that this was in Ikebukuro somewhere.

The swings on the swingset began to rock; a shadow appeared upon them.

"......"

The shadow got darker and darker over time, taking the form of a human girl wearing a wide-brimmed hat. After a few creaking swings back and forth, her form steadily vanished.

Shinra watched the video with great fascination. The shadow lines coming from the feet of the girl-shaped shadow stretched longer and longer, reaching toward the camera until they extended out of the frame.

"...This is your shadow, right?" he pointed out.

Celty promptly flinched. She covered the place where her human face would have been with her hands and began to roll back and forth on the rug.

"*Waaaah! Shinra, I'm the worst! It doesn't matter if I was desperate, I can't just shoot a video of some staged paranormal phenomenon and upload it to Niconico!*"

"Calm down, Celty. Okay? Listen up. Yes, you created that phenomenon yourself, but just so we're clear, your shadow is actually way more paranormal than some little glimpse of a ghost, all right? So in a sense, you're not actually lying to anyone. It's more like you're filming yourself dancing, or..."

"*It's all over. If anyone finds out I made this video, they're going to realize it was all faked, and they're going to tear me apart, and I'll be forced to go on the news and apologize in a live press confereeeence!"*

"Celty. Calm down. Celty."

She continued rolling back and forth, wildly typing deranged thoughts into her phone.

"But then, when it comes time for the apology, I'm going to get the wrong idea and think, 'Being aggressive makes me seem full of myself,' and then I'll make it a really off-putting and sarcastic apology with jokes that just make everyone even madder, and after the conference is over, I'm going to forget that the mic is still on and start having a really embarrassing conversation with you that everyone's going to hearrrrrrr! Aaaaaahhhhhh! It's all over! What do I do, Shinra?!"

"Um, to address your points in order, first of all, the 'staged' aspect of your video is not quite the same as the 'staged' videos people label on Niconico, okay? Also, why would you have a live apology press conference? You can't even talk. Are you going to continually apologize with uploader comments in a banner at the top of the video? Also, even if you forget to turn the mic off after the conference, you realize the only thing people are going to hear is my voice, right?"

He paused there for a breath, then continued, looking more serious this time.

"Of course, I'll admit that I'm incredibly curious about what kind of conversation we might be having that would be so embarrassing. Perhaps you could tell me more about that fantasy?"

"W-well, it would be things we normally talk about, but just more embarrassing because other people would hear them."

"Oh, you've got it bad. Normally, you would have hit me in the kidneys for asking something like that, but since you just answered it normally, you must really be up against the wall right now."

He reached out to stroke Celty's trembling shoulder, trying to comfort his beloved.

"Look, you shouldn't worry about this. Even if all of that does happen, I'll still be the last person on your side."

"But then I'll be ruining your life…"

"No, I'll be fine. I'll do anything for you—inflating view counts, adding bookmarks, whatever you want! I'm happy being the one to do all the dirty work, as long as you cleanse my spoiled heart with the power of your love! Wow, now that I mention it, that's basically a perfect plan, isn't it?!"

"Umm…"

"Come, Celty! Subscribe to my private Niconico channel and attach the 'adults only' tag to my life!"

"Uh, hang on."

After a few seconds of thought, Celty delivered a powerful counterpunch to Shinra's torso when he tried to leap onto her.

Several minutes later…

"Thank you, Shinra. I feel much calmer now."

"Uh…don't mention it… This is the Celty…I'd much rather see…"

While Celty had calmed down, Shinra was giving a thumbs-up with a heavy sheen of nervous sweat on his face.

"A-are you all right? Sorry, I was really wound up, so I might not have held back…"

"I'm perfectly fine! The pain from you punching me is just more evidence that we've had physical contact!"

"Are you sure you're all right? You didn't hit your head, or…?"

"Of course! If anything, my head is clearer than ever. It's helped me come up with a good idea," Shinra said, smiling dazzlingly. He turned to the laptop screen.

It was playing back the "Patrol Officer vs. Headless Rider" video on Niconico.

He said, "The person who filmed and submitted this was Karisawa's rival…umm…"

"Blizzard La Blizzardia."

"Yes, Bli-what's-her-name's friend, correct?"

"That's right, supposedly…"

Shinra glanced out of the corner of his eye at Celty's text, then adjusted the time slider to stop the video at a particular point.

"See here, when Shooter is trying to escape into the air…for just a brief moment, he's pointed straight at the camera, right?"

"Oh! You're right!"

"Meaning that at this moment…the camera mounted in Shooter's headlight position should show you the person who submitted this video."

"…! I see!" Celty remarked, feeling positive at first, but she soon racked her nonexistent brain to find the answer to a question that occurred to her. "But assuming that is what happened…what then?"

"Well, if we're able to identify who the person is, then we might get closer to this Blizzard-whoever. Then you can get in the middle and convince them both to stop this stupid video competition! Basically, you just need to help Karisawa and her rival make up!"

"Ah, I see! But…I have a feeling it's not going to be that easy…," Celty said nervously.

Shinra busied himself with checking Celty's video and comparing the two.

"Don't worry. We've already got a leg up on them; they were filming my Celty without permission. As long as we can worm our way into a conversation using that, it should work out."

"Don't think I didn't catch that 'my.'"

"Ah, but more importantly, I've found the filmer!" Shinra shouted, loudly and obviously, pointing at the screen. "Look, right there… wait… Haven't I seen this kid before…?"

"Where…? Oh?!"

Right there was the image of a boy, pointing his smartphone camera at the screen.

And it was a face Celty recognized.

"That's…Aoba Kuronuma!"

"…He's come to our place before, hasn't he?" There was a cold, eerie light in Shinra's eyes. "He said he wanted to be friends, but then he secretly films you while you were afraid, and shows it to the entire world… I guess I *should've* sliced his carotid artery back then, shouldn't I?"

"Don't be macabre!" Celty scolded him.

I can't believe it was Aoba, she thought. *Which would mean that his friend…Blizzard La Blizzardia must be a Blue Square? No…I'm pretty sure Blizzard La Blizzardia is female. And now that I think of it, I don't think I actually took a careful look at her videos.*

Celty searched the tags on Nico Video, and decided to actually search out the videos of the masked singer and rival of Erika Karisawa's Eternal de Charmonte.

…She's…

…actually pretty good at singing and dancing.

But…

It was a girl dressed in a rather provocative style with a mask, dancing and singing. It wasn't an idol-style dance, but something like out of a particularly dark musical play.

I don't know what it is, but she looks familiar, too…

Shinra peered over her shoulder and remarked, "Oh, isn't that..."

"*You know her, Shinra?*"

"Yes, and you know her too," he said, so casually that it came as a surprise to her. "This is Izaya's little sister, Kururi."

♂♀

The next day, parking lot, Ikebukuro

"...Now, I know you weren't seriously fighting over this, but you gotta keep yourself from dragging others into the bullshit," Kyouhei Kadota growled with disappointment. Karisawa and Kururi were standing side by side before him and lowering their heads with shame.

"Heh-heh-heh...sorree, Dotachin."

"...Apology..." [I'm sorry.]

Kadota was a mutual acquaintance of both and had called them here to bring an end to the nonsense that had involved Celty and others. When she learned the truth, she asked Kadota to be a go-between and get the entire video contest between the two nullified.

"I'm sorry, Kururi. I wasn't being very mature."

"...Same..." [Me, neither.]

The two girls decided to settle the matter by joining together and collaborating on a special Niconico live stream.

And at last, Celty was freed from the heavy responsibility of being a content creator.

♂♀

Days later, Shinra's apartment

"Hey, the Nico stream's about to start!" Shinra called out.

Celty moved in front of the computer to watch. On the stream, an oddly decorated table was host to a masked Karisawa and the Orihara sisters.

"Hi, I'm Eternal de Charmonte."

"..."

"And I'll speak for my reticent sister! Hey y'all! We're Blizzard La Blizzardia and her little sister, Flame!"

"*Mairu's stage name is not nearly as fancy as the others,*" Celty remarked in text to Shinra. *"I can't believe it never occurred to me... I ran into her in town not that long ago, and she told me about the videos she did with her sister..."*

"I checked out the entry for Blizzard La Blizzardia on the Niconico Encyclopedia, and it does say that 'they often perform extreme dances, and a video in which she danced with her masked little sister was once deleted.'"

"Do they ever get tired of riling people up?"

Now that she was free of the pressure to produce a video, Celty felt much more relaxed watching this stream.

"You know, it's weird... Part of it is that I'd almost never heard her voice before this, but it's really wild to think that such a quiet and reserved girl can sing and dance like that."

"Well, Kururi gets extremely loquacious and provocative in online chats," Shinra noted sagely. "Plus, on a site like Nico Video, you can show off a side of yourself that you don't usually display. Sometimes the person you show off in your videos is more like your ideal self."

"I see."

"Plus, some viewers look up to them. When singers and dancers are really popular, they either have to live pure and upright lives themselves, or maintain a healthy distance from their fans."

"What's your point?" Celty asked.

Shinra's features broke into a smile. "You work as an underground courier, and you don't have the option of putting yourself at a distance from others. So I hope that rather than becoming some video idol, you stick to being *my* idol."

Celty's shoulders bobbed up and down in the gesture of a sigh. She ran her fingers over the tablet.

"You stole my line, black-market doctor."

Then she leaned so that her shoulder touched his, and the moment was just right.

Until the masked girls on the screen began to say things that completely destroyed the mood.

"So, as a sign of our reconciliation, the three of us have decided to do live commentary on a game."

"……"

"Yeah! And I brought a game that almost no one has ever heard of!" said the girl who looked like Mairu, waving a CD-ROM with her hand.

The top surface of the CD-ROM had the words *State of Affairs, Izaya's Castle etc.* written on it in marker.

"This is a game that our brother made, ages ago! And we're going to show it on-screen and talk over it!"

No...

With a silent cry, Celty frantically typed out a stream comment and slammed the cursor over the submit button.

"Not that game! Anything but that game!"

That comment, an inexplicable scream to a total stranger, was Celty's very first live comment on a Nico stream.

This is a comment tale.

A tale of twisted comments.

♂♀

After a number of smaller, personal incidents and events like this, Celty and Shinra left Ikebukuro for a time to go on a journey around all of Japan.

It was a long trip that took half a year. How did it change Celty—or not change her, as the case may have been? Even she couldn't tell you.

Nor did she know what they would see when they returned after six months.

Or whether or not the Headless Rider could continue to smile…

The answer would not arrive until slightly later.

Fin

INTERMISSION E

After nearly two hours of looking at photographs and chatting, Celty decided to take a bit of a break.

"You know," she said to Shinra, *"once you start looking at photos, there's no place to stop. The memories are just endless."*

"It's a sign of how rich our days have been. Of course, I don't need photos at all—I can simply close my eyes and remember everything in vivid detail!"

"...The scary part is that your memories are full of major elaborations and fantasies..."

"Oh, come now, Celty," Shinra said, staring right at her, his cheeks red. "They're my memories. Surely I should be allowed to embellish them."

"Don't act like you're so principled! Remember, these are my memories, too!" Celty snapped back.

Shinra's face lit up. "Celty...so you're saying that your memories with me *are* important to you, too?!"

"Uh, well, I didn't..." She fumbled around for a bit before glancing at the computer again, hoping to find a distraction. *"Hey, let's check out some more photos."*

"Come on, you can't fool me, Celty!" He watched the screen with her, beaming, then noticed a green photo in the corner of the viewing list. "What's that one?"

He pressed it on the touch-sensitive screen of the laptop, opening it up.

At first glance, it seemed to be nothing more than a joke, but Shinra, who was a part of it, was smiling with a different expression than usual.

"Ahh, this one…"

It was a very strange picture of Celty with a watermelon on her head. They traded some very nostalgic words.

"Ohh, I remember this. That was… Well, it all feels like a dream now."

"It sure does," Shinra said, lifting the corners of his mouth in a soft smile and casting a warm glance at Celty.

"It really was like a dream, in many ways."

Warning! Warning! The following story is a crossover with author Ryohgo Narita's story *Vamp!* Also, be warned that, as this story was published in a parody-themed collection, Yumasaki and Karisawa's Dengeki Bunko nerdery is even more intense than usual.

SIDE STORY 8
DURAMP!! AVOIDING LOVE IN THE CENTER OF THE WORLD

It was a clearly abnormal thing.

Months after the Night of the Ripper, when Saika deluged the streets of Ikebukuro, the city welcomed another fantastical being. Ikebukuro had been getting used to Saika and the Headless Rider, but this was something different.

Something clearly not human.

A grotesque creature beyond the realm of common sense.

What did this vision portend for Ikebukuro?

This is a fantastical tale.

A tale of a dreaming fantasy.

♂♀

This is a nice city. Very nice.
This place called Tokyo is so full of desires.
It's not at all like that island in Germany.
That's right. Maybe here…
Maybe here I can suck up all the power I want.
I can gain strength here.
My desire will overwhelm all the desire of this city.
Ha-ha-ha-ha-ha, ha-ha-ha-ha-ha-ha-ha-ha-ha-ha-ha…

♂♀

Evening, Kawagoe Highway, top floor of apartment building

"Well, thanks, Celty. Now I'm covered in crab omelet."

"*Shut up.*"

Shinra Kishitani sat there with soft-boiled yellow yolk dripping down his head, earning him a cold rebuke from his lover.

The message had been typed and displayed on the screen of the PDA in Celty Sturluson's hand.

Celty didn't have a voice—because she didn't have eyes, a nose, mouth, ears, or *any part of a head at all.*

She was a type of fairy commonly known as a dullahan, and originally lived in Europe, but was currently forced to wander around Tokyo in search of her missing head.

Now she was living out of the home of the black-market doctor she had chosen for a life partner, and for the moment it was a mutually reciprocated relationship. That did not mean that they were equally sappy toward each other, however.

"Heh-heh-heh. I feel I've suffered the slings and arrows of outrageous fortune, but I still forgive you. I do bear some responsibility for saying nonsense, after all."

Perhaps they had been in some kind of fight, with the way crab omelet was splattered over Shinra's head, but he smiled as he wiped it off.

"*Just stop talking,*" Celty said, as if she was shaking the head that wasn't there. She walked to the window.

With the setting sun casting its light over the city before her, the headless girl began a mental monologue.

My head may have vanished into the wind...but I can still feel its presence. It's still here, somewhere in Tokyo...

Though she did not have the same fixation on it as before, she was still curious about its location. She stood silently at the window and allowed her nerves to sharpen, searching out into the city at night as far as the eye could see.

The shadow that wound itself around her body sensed the presence of something alien in the vicinity. It was somewhere distant—the signal was faded—but she could indeed feel her head out there.

But on this day, there was also something else.

Huh?

"What is it, Celty?"

Alert to the change in her mood, Shinra rushed over to her, quickly wiping the crab omelet from his clothes with a towel.

While she kept her attention on the window, Celty typed a brief message to her lover on the PDA.

"Something's in the city."

"Like what?"

"I feel it keenly. Something else that's not human. Something like me." She was typing rapidly.

Shinra's eyes narrowed behind his glasses.

"...You don't think it's another dullahan, do you?"

"No, it's not. This feels more…sludgy. It's something I remember. I've felt presences like this a number of times in the past."

She delved into the memory of her body, not her head, to recall a particular being.

"This feels like…"

She paused, hesitating, then struck the keys—putting a very conflicted look on Shinra's face.

"A succubus."

♂♀

Human beings are built from desire.

It is why they have prospered to the extent that they have.

And I am something greater, something that feeds upon their prosperity.

Just the thought of that status fulfills me.

Wait and see, Viscount. You will not treat me like some lowly maid much longer.

I will gain a power in this town that no one can surpass. And then I will take over your island.

Oh, strength has nothing to do with it.

As long as I can control desire, I am invincible. Even the most powerful being in the entire world will be under my command if I wield their desires…

However, with so much desire all around, you would think that others of my kind would be nearby…

Hmm. Either they don't know about this place, or they have no interest in Japan… That is their loss. All the more for me. It was worth sucking that Japanese knowledge out of Mamiya.

* * *

Now, let's start with a little prep work.

There do seem to be many people in this city that are very ostentatious and frivolous. I'd rather start with a more innocent soul...

...I'm not seeing any.

But there are so many people here. I've got every flavor I could possibly want.

Hmm...those three going into that restaurant, the two boys and one girl... One of them seems eager for attention...but the other two look very innocent and pure, indeed.

They seem so plain, and most of all, young.

So, what kind of dream shall I give to these boys and girl in the prime of their youth...?

♂♀

Inside a restaurant, Sixtieth Floor Street, Ikebukuro

Inside the major chain family restaurant on the second floor of this particular building, Mikado Ryuugamine glanced over the menu he'd been given.

The restaurant was almost completely full, and he and his two friends sat down at a table by the window.

"I'm kinda hungry. What should I have?"

Mikado and the girl across from him, Anri Sonohara, wore the uniform jackets of a high school in the area, while the other boy sitting next to Mikado, Masaomi Kida, had on a bright and stylish personal outfit that looked natural on him.

"I've already got my order. Hey, waitress! C'mon, baby!"

"Please don't embarrass us!" Mikado pleaded, face already red.

Anri watched the two with a warm smile.

Mikado and Anri were the two student council representatives for the class, and Mikado currently had an unrequited crush on her. Or maybe it was requited, but Mikado hadn't been able to confirm that for himself.

The reason for that was sitting next to him, flapping the menu to blow air on Mikado.

"You know, when we sit in this configuration, it looks just like we're in a love triangle, huh? And I'm already tired of the will-they-won't-they tension. So you can go now, Mikado. Scram!"

"What are you talking about?!" Mikado protested, wide-eyed.

Masaomi just shook his head. "What…? Are you saying you *like* this ugly, festering love triangle situation? *Sigh*… And here I thought you were the perennial virgin prude who remains pure at heart forever. Turns out you're actually a stone cold erorist."

"Erorist…?"

"You erotic fiend. You eronster. And let me be clear: *ero* is a higher level than *ecchi*. I mean, *ecchi* is just a derivation of H, the initial for *hentai*. That's a provincial Japan-only term. But consider the refined, international ring of *eros*! Look at you. You're a world-class erotic eroustabout! I've heard that love has no boundaries. Now you're telling me that horny has no national borders, either?!"

"Stop saying that word in a restaurant!" Mikado demanded, blushing deeply.

Fortunately, the other patrons were too busy with their own conversations to notice Masaomi's total lack of propriety, so no one else was paying attention to them.

Despite Mikado's relief, Masaomi turned to Anri across the table and continued, "You can't do this, Anri. Anri, don't be like this. This erobot is after your body. Hang around with a randy lad like this and you'll end up naked. He's stolen something quite precious: your body."

"Umm…"

Anri didn't know how to react to this. She just looked uncomfortable.

"I, on the other hand, am very safe. First, the only thing I'm getting naked is your heart. *Tu corazón, señorita. ¿Cómo estás? Muy bien.*"

"Umm…"

"I can't believe you can say that stuff with a straight face," Mikado interjected, trying to help out the blushing Anri. He fixed his booth partner with an icy stare.

It didn't have the tiniest effect on Masaomi, however. He watched a waitress walk past and started guessing her measurements.

"I'm gonna say 33, 26, 34 inches."

"Yeah, which of us is the pervert, again? Oh, hang on…gotta use the restroom."

As Mikado got up, Masaomi wore a lecherous smile and called out, "Hee-hee-hee! You sure you wanna do that? While you're in the bathroom, Anri and I are gonna elope to indulge our passions!"

Mikado completely ignored him and vanished into the men's room.

* * *

"He *is* a good guy at heart," Mikado said into the mirror as he washed his hands.

The thought of the earlier conversation put a self-deprecating smile on his lips. Masaomi was not actually putting any moves on Anri. He acted that way around just about any woman who met his fancy.

In other words, Masaomi was not, in fact, a direct romantic rival. However, when he made these jokes and comments, it made it that much more difficult for Mikado to admit his affections for Anri.

A part of him thought it would be better just to man up and tell her his feelings to get it over with, but he had a feeling that whether she turned him down or they started going out officially, it would not affect Masaomi's behavior whatsoever.

But there was a problem to solve before he got to that…

"I don't even know if I can ask Sonohara out. If Kida doesn't do it first…"

Masaomi had been calling her by her first name, Anri, from the very start, which was extremely forward. But Mikado still called her Sonohara.

"It's no good…"

He cursed his own shyness and stared into his eyes in the mirror.

He saw his face, weak and submissive.

And behind it, Anri's.

"?!"

He flinched and spun around, staring into the wide-open eyes of the girl standing before him.

"S-S-Sonohara! W-what's going on? D-did you already order for me?" he asked stupidly, so confused and panicked that he momentarily forgot he was in the men's room.

But at the same time, he realized something was off about the girl with him.

She had been wearing her school jacket moments ago, but now, for some reason, she had taken it off, so that she wore only her shirt and skirt. The restaurant wasn't particularly warm, and she had been wearing it when he got up from the table just a minute earlier.

Before he could think any more about what this meant, Anri giggled softly and raised a hand to her chest.

"Mikado…"

"Huh?"

"While Kida may have said all that…stuff earlier…the truth is that I don't mind…if you're a little…*ecchi*."

"Huh?!"

Mikado was so taken aback by this that he froze in place. He didn't really understand what she was saying, but he was very, very aware that she was reaching up to undo the buttons on her shirt.

"W-wait…So-So-Sono-Sono-Sonohara?!" he gasped, panicking.

Anri's hands slid over her shirt. With each descent, the white shirt opened further, revealing more and more pale, smooth skin.

"I'd be fine…if it's with you…"

"Whaaaaaaat?"

He was beside himself with confusion. Bit by bit, first teasingly, then occasionally boldly, Anri removed her clothing. When all the buttons of her shirt were undone, it revealed skin like porcelain and a white bra nearly the same color.

"U-um, Sonohara?! What's the matter?! Did you start playing truth or dare with Kida while I was away?!" he fretted.

Anri just blushed slightly, then reached around her back.

"Wha—no! You can't be serious!"

But Mikado's guess was correct: she was reaching to undo the hook on her bra.

Helpless to stop it, helpless to look away or directly at her, Mikado felt himself back into the sink. He was trapped.

At the same time, there was an oddly rational and alert part of his brain that thought, *Oh, when she takes off her clothes with the glasses still on—something about that is extremely hot.*

Just then, the door of the restroom clicked open, and Masaomi entered the room, humming a merry tune.

"Aaaaaah!" Mikado promptly shouted, much to Masaomi's confusion.

"What are you doing? Your face is red, man… Are you feeling sick?"

"Huh? Huh?"

It was then that Mikado realized that he and Masaomi were the only people in the restroom.

"Wh-where's Sonohara?"

"Huh? She's just sitting at the table… Oh, I get it. You're hoping to play while the cat's away, huh?!"

Mikado ignored him, pushed the door back open, and returned to the restaurant. At the table by the window, Anri was sitting there, wiping her hands with the provided moist towelette.

She hadn't even taken off her jacket, much less her shirt. Everything was exactly the way it had been when Mikado had gotten up from the table.

"???"

Now he was thoroughly scrambled on the inside, but his outside tried awkwardly to play it cool and get him to his seat.

"U-um, Sonohara…"

"Yes?"

"…Uh, n-nothing."

"What's the matter, Ryuugamine?" she asked, mystified. But this helped Mikado realize something.

Back there, she called me "Mikado"…

Normally Anri always called him Ryuugamine. It was perhaps a little overly reserved for them both to call each other by their last names at this point, but given their respective personalities, it felt rather natural for them to do so.

So what the heck was that version of her?

It was much too vivid to be a simple hallucination, and more importantly, he had no idea why he would be having a hallucination at all.

Anri had definitely been present in the restroom, but it felt as though he was the only one seeing her. The reality of the situation had been tenuous at best. Maybe he would have felt her breath if he'd been close enough, but maybe his hand would have passed right through her if he'd reached out.

Almost like he'd been dreaming while awake…

♂♀

Heh-heh-heh.

Ha-ha-ha-ha-ha-ha-ha.

This is fun.

Quite delightful, in fact.

Yes, I was interrupted just before I sucked the vitality from him, but seducing humans of that sort always makes my heart dance and sing.

Only my designated target can actually see me. Such is the power of succubi and other demons of the night. And when we reveal ourselves to that target, they do not see us as we truly are.

We did not reach the stage of congress—but I did gain a foothold using him. Now I can sense the desires of any person with a connection to that boy, whether in his vicinity or not. I can sense the color and size of the desires harbored in any soul within the memory of his soul—and I can fly to them whenever I want.

Choosing the first person in a new land is a crucial task, but it would seem that I chose correctly with that youth. For all his apparent innocence and diffidence, he has quite a number of connections to others. And I feel that almost all of them are here in this city.

This is good. It means that I will be able to reap a tremendous amount of vitality and essence in a short amount of time.

The viscount, the maids, the werewolves…in fact, even that detestable relict will all be inferior to the power I will find here.

Heh-heh-heh. First I'll start with the powerful desire I feel in that nearby park. Let's see what you have to offer…

♂♀

Minami-Ikebukuro Park

"Here it comes, Seiji! Open wide!"

"Th…thanks, Mika."

Heh-heh-heh, there they are. The man and woman sitting on that bench… Yes, I can tell that they're exuding some very powerful desire.

I'll imprint the man's desire onto my body and tear apart the connection he has with her. That might be fun.

And after I've drained the life force from him, I'll turn my attention on the lovelorn woman and take hers as well.

Now let's take a look at the kind of desire that exists in his soul…

……
Wh—   It looks like…

A head?!

            *　*　*

A severed head?!

Th-the vision of desire within this man's being...the image that is flooding into my mind—cannot be anything else!
And...and it's the head of the woman he's with!
W-what's wrong with this man?
Are his tastes so abnormal?!
Damn. I saw plenty of sadomasochism and fetishes in my homeland, but I've never seen someone whose desires are so outright dangerous!
Is he some kind of sick serial killer or something?!
Oh no. I need to send her some kind of warning, I suppose.
No, I'm a demon of the night. I have no obligation to help this human woman.
Gods below, but the strength of his desire is off the charts!
If only it were a more healthy sexual desire, it would be the ideal source of power for me...but if I devour this wish of his, it will only twist my own strength as well.
Hmm. What about the woman, though?
I suppose she's brimming with desire for this man. Maybe I can use that to...
......
Wait.
Not so fast.
Yes, her desire is in regards to the man.
But there's not an ounce of sexuality to it. All she feels is the desire for pure control.
...And maybe a bit of love, too...? It's so wrapped up in the need for control, it's hard to tell.
What kind of relationship are these people in?
Hmm, I sense another kind of powerful desire within the woman...

The instant I saw it, I vanished from the park.
Absolutely not. I was not going to stay there a moment longer.
Not in a place of such twisted desires.
The other desire I saw in her—the visual that came into my head—was taking the severed head that looked like her, grinding it into a paste, and putting it into her own mouth... Ugh, I can't even stand to remember it.

What a bunch of freaks.
I feel sick just looking at them.
From what I hear, there are other night demons that specialize in dreams of that sort, but I'll have no part in it.
The people on that island in Germany might have smaller desires, but their wishes are at least neater and colored in an appealing way.
Very well. I'll have to try my luck elsewhere.
The sun still hasn't gone all the way down yet, and there are still many connections to that boy's soul to choose from.
…Ooh, I sense another human with a powerful desire very close by.
Perhaps this will be a good palate cleanser. I'll devour the greedy desires that fill this city!
Kwa-ha-ha-ha-ha-ha-ha-ha…

♂♀

Outside of Seibu Dept. Store, Ikebukuro

My, there are so many people in this city.
 It's nothing at all like that rural island.
 But the presence of non-human beings is rather scarce.

Ah, here we go.
Hmph. He might be wearing sunglasses, but this man seems rather timid. Since he has a connection to that boy somehow, I'll assume he should be a pushover.
Then I shall do as I did with that Mikado youth earlier and take the form of the object of his desire.
Let us see what this man wants…

…A man?

Oh? Is he homosexual?
That's fine. Love comes in all forms, after all.
I'm starting to get a little hungry, though. And some passion among men every now and again is a nice change of pace.
From what I've heard, the desire in same-sex relationships can be even deeper and more turbulent.
Well, now that I know the plan…

* * *

"Hey."

I transformed into the figure the man in the sunglasses desired most and stood before him, grinning.

No one else could see me but the man in the sunglasses. Unlike with that Mikado boy earlier, there would be no interruption this time. I'd have a chance to lure him somewhere and...

"Iiizaaayaaa..."

Hah! Look at that grin. He has no idea I'm a fake.

Once he's opened up his heart to me, I'll read all the information I need about the man I'm impersonating, right out of his head. It would be easier if I could read all that information before transforming, but I don't quite have the power I need yet.

He just has to open himself to me, and then...

"I've been dying to see you. I wanted to see you so bad, Izayaaaa..."

Hmm? Strange. He's still not opening his heart to merglalbryuaƎΞ‡——

"I gotta tell ya, I've been tearin' my hair out over here, Izayaaaaa! It's been killing me that I couldn't pound you into a fine dust!"

Oh no.

This isn't love!

This man was just thinking about another man he wanted to punch!

By the time I realized my mistake, however, the man with the sunglasses grabbed my collar before I could undo the illusion—and hurled me straight up into the air.

For a brief moment, the ground was far below me.

My wings—I have to deploy my wings!

I have to show my true nature, extend my wings, and fly off before I hit the ground...

It'll mean showing myself to this man, since he's still my target, but there's no helping that now-how-how-how-ha-ha-ha-haaaaaaaa—

"You really do have the best timing in every situation, don't ya?! It pisses me off, in fact!"

An impact ran through my body.

The man in the sunglasses had leapt up to chase after me, then slammed me into the asphalt like he was dunking a basketball.

He landed cleanly, then lifted one foot high over his head.

Fool! I'm a succubus. Your human kicks can't—

"Die."

Gwah?!
"Die."
Wait...no...
"Die."
How does he hit so hard?!
"Die."
This has to be even more powerful than the vampires at the castle—
"Die."
He must be tired of kicking, because now he's straddling me to punch my faceghrblh!
"Die."
G-g-g-gotta undo my ap-ap-ap-appearance...
"Die."
C-c-c-can't do it, the pain and force keeps me from concentra...
"Die." *I, I, I'm dying!*
"Die." *Dying!*
"Die." *Dying!*
"Die."
H-h-help, help me, s-s-s-somebody—

♂♀

A large man approached Shizuo Heiwajima from behind, while Shizuo himself straddled me.

"Hi, Shizuuuo. What you doing?"

"Die-die-die-die... Huh? What do you want, Simon? It's weird, Izaya just doesn't have the same mettle as usual. I was gonna just go ahead and hit him a hundred times until he dies..."

"But Izaya is eating sushi in our restaurant right now."

"Huh?"

This message from Simon, the Black man in the sushi chef's apron, took Shizuo aback. He looked up, then back at his feet.

"...Huh?"

"Looks like a bundle of rags."

"...So who's this, then?"

"Dunno."

Simon glanced at the succubus, which was no longer capable of hiding itself from others, and shook his head.

Until just moments ago, it had worn the face of Izaya Orihara, but now that face was so swollen that it was barely even recognizable as belonging to a human.

"H-hey…"

Now Shizuo was glancing around awkwardly. He slowly got off the night demon and reached out.

"Hy…hyaaaiiiighh!"

The succubus shrieked and got to its feet, then bolted off with inhuman speed into the crowd.

"…?"

"Oooh. It was fast— Could be Izaya after all," said Simon. He and Shizuo shared a look, then muttered to themselves.

"…Was that a doppelgänger or something? I didn't get the wrong guy, did I?"

"That's strange… Shizuo was punching empty ground and yelling. Why that person show up there…?"

♂♀

Junkudo Books, Ikebukuro

"Motorrad. Parentheses, note: A two-wheeled vehicle. Refers only to those who do not fly, close parentheses."

Of all the bookstores in Japan, Junkudo was one of the largest.

In a section of the basement level full of manga, novels for young adults, and various subculture magazines, a young man with sharp eyes and a large backpack muttered to himself.

"What's up, Yumacchi? You even said the parentheses out loud," noted the surprised woman next to him.

As if on cue, the young man said loudly, "Then what is a two-wheeled vehicle that *does* fly called?!"

She caught the book that he tossed into the air, and exclaimed, "Oh nooo! Yumacchi's snapped!"

The man she called "Yumacchi," who was actually Walker Yumasaki, waved a hand around with no care for any attention he might be gathering. "Ugh, I'm just so jealous of this motorrad! Getting to ride all over the land with this adorable girl named Kino on its back! It's not fair!"

"Calm down, Yumacchi! In that world, they just call flying two-wheeled vehicles 'bikes'! It said so somewhere!" said his partner,

Karisawa, who was desperately trying and failing to calm Yumasaki's ranting.

"Oooh... Minami gets to be a double heroine in both *Dokuro-chan* and *Binkan the Sensitive Salaryman*! What the heck?! Are they trying to shunt Minami's fans toward a different series?! Waaaah! Our poor Minami!"

"Hey! What's wrong? You're acting weird today, Yumacchi!"

It was at this point that Yumasaki finally looked at Karisawa.

"The group chat...and maids."

"What?"

"...See, there's this foreigner I met through online chat, right? And it turns out, it turns out, he's freeloading at this rich family's house! He gets to sleep and wake up under the same r-roof as m-m-maids... So many maiiiiiiiiids!"

"...Ahhh..."

Karisawa felt that she had figured out the situation. Just then, a third person entered the picture.

"Hey, don't cause a scene at the bookstore."

"Ah, sorry, Dotachin. Yumacchi was having one of his fits! It's been a while."

"Again, huh?"

Dotachin, better known as Kadota, sighed and began to put back the books he'd pulled off the shelves. "Listen, Yumasaki, just because Junkudo is a big store doesn't mean you should be shouting at the top of your lungs."

"I'm not shouting! I'm just letting out air so that my heart doesn't burst! Arrrgh, why don't I have any maaaaids?! I know there are guys in the real world who are living out all the 2D fantasies! It's not fair!"

"For not having any interest at all in 3D girls, he sure does get jealous over 2D-like situations. And the few times he really snaps, it turns out like this..."

"This is such a pain in the ass," Kadota grumbled.

Yumasaki continued to wail with self-pity, rolling around on the floor of the bookstore.

"Yes, yes, of course, of course! I can't get off to 3D girls! But when you hear about a situation involving maids, you usually think of 2D first, don't you?! Ugh! Why can't 3D be 2D?! No matter how rich I might become, the dream will never come true!"

"Can you just shut him up already, Karisawa? The other customers and employees are really glaring at us."

She sighed and nodded. More harshly than usual, she said, "Yumacchi."

"Huh?"

"If you don't pipe down now, I'm going to tell you *all the endings* of this month's new Dengeki Bunko releases."

Yumasaki immediately froze in place on the floor where he'd been rolling. "N-no, don't! I just bought them today; I haven't read them yet!"

"Well, I bought them this morning, and I've read them all. Oh, who could have guessed that—"

Yumasaki was promptly in a groveling position, rubbing his forehead on the floor and wailing, "I'm sorry, I got a little carried away! I won't defy you again, I won't yell and shout, I'll behave, so *please* don't do that! Anything but that, anything, anything, anything…"

"We still have some books to check out, so you stay out here and cool your jets a little!"

In the end, they took Yumasaki outside and tossed him into Togusa's van, which was parked in the lot. The driver himself seemed to have gone off on his own.

"Rrrgh! I'll admit, I wondered if two-wheeled vehicles that fly really *are* a thing. But the Black Rider practically swims from wall to wall, right…? Once you've seen that for yourself…you can't help but hold tight to a faint hope, can't you?!"

Left behind in the rear of the van, Yumasaki continued to vent and roll around on the floor.

"Aaaah! Maids are so great, great are the maids. Like Wilhelmina in *Shana*. In fact, you could give me someone like Domino, I don't care—I just want a maid!" he wailed, compromising with a character that was not, strictly speaking, a maid.

Yumasaki glanced out of the van window in boredom and noticed a man dressed in familiar clothes, face swollen, walking unsteadily.

"Huh? Isn't that…Izaya?"

♂♀

How can this be?

Thanks to that man earlier, I've had to completely expend all of my stamina.

For now, I need to recover...

I don't care who it is now. In fact, I'd even take that pair with the severed head earlier. I'll show them the illusions they want to see. Anything to get a bit of their power...

"Is that you, Izaya?"

"W-what's this?"

"What happened to you? You look dreadful..."

The door on a nearby car opened, and a man came out, rushing toward me.

Ah, so he must recognize the man whose form I'm currently using.

...Oh? And he's got ties to that Mikado boy as well...

Plus, it seems that he's feeling incredibly unsatisfied at the moment.

Well, this is it. If I can manage to use him...

"Come on, let's get you into the car, then."

"Ah, ah..."

With hardly any strength left at my disposal, I couldn't stop the man from dragging me to his car and pushing me inside.

"What's the matter with you? Did you have another fight with Shizuo? If that's true, it's rare to see you get beaten so badly," he said.

The door shut behind me, and I was trapped in something like a private cell. The rear seat had been taken out of the car, so it was much more spacious inside than you would think from the outside.

I was no longer able to vanish, but I could still at least cause the other man to hallucinate.

Somehow I have to look into his mind and see his desires...

...Ugh, this is how weakened I've become. I can't even get a good look inside.

Well, at this point, I might as well...

While the man looked away, I transformed into a pinup photo model that I'd seen recently in a magazine.

"Hey," I called out, in the sexiest and most inviting voice I could possibly produce.

"Huh...? Whoa?! Izaya just transformed into a lady in a swimsuit!"

While he panicked, I leaned forward and looked upward at him as I sidled closer.

"Wait, am I dreaming right now?" He pinched his cheek.

I said, in my most seductive whisper, "That's right...it is a dream. And that means you can do *anything* you want to me..."

Despite being a demon of seduction, however, I still didn't feel entirely comfortable with this kind of feminine mannerism. I'd spent too much time at that damned viscount's place.

At any rate, first things first: I had to suck the vitality from this man. *Now get aroused! Allow your passions to be open and enflamed...*

...H-huh?

That's weird. Why do his eyes look so cold and flat?

"Wow...I must be more exhausted than I realized."

"Huh...?"

"If I'm actually dreaming of a 3D photo model, I've got it bad... At this point, I might be up for some enjoyable chitchat in 3D, but only if she were in cosplay. This? Just a bikini model? It's terminal... I'm so cooked. I need sleep."

The man promptly lay down inside the van.

He ignored me.

He ignored me!

I felt incredibly insulted and wounded.

I had to drag him down into a frenzy of physical lust. I had to capture him and draw out the lifeforce until he was dead!

"Hey! Get up!"

"What do you waaant? If you're a dream, wait until I'm asleep to show up."

"Shuddup! My pride as a succubus is at stake! I'll transform into whatever you desire! And it'll allow me to feed on your life force! I'll do whatever it takes!" I said, frustrated enough to be brutally frank about it.

That was a mistake. If I tell him I'm a succubus, he's going to be even more certain that this is a dream.

"...Succubus."

But his reaction was not what I expected.

"...Succubus."

Without getting up, he slowly lifted his hand to his cheek, and pinched as hard as it seemed possible to do.

"...Ouch. That hurts so much. So it's not a dream."

Instantly, like a spring-loaded puppet, he leapt to his feet, right inside the car.

"Succubuuuus!"

"Aaaaaaah!!"

This alarmed me, and it was all I could do just to maintain my bikini model appearance.

"Succubus?! Is that what I think it is?! The kind that appear in the dreams of holy figures and cause them to sink into depravity, so that you can absorb their vitality and give birth to more of your kind?!"

"How do you know so much?!"

But I am not the kind that he just described. I cannot go into people's dreams. Some of them might, but I am the sort that removes my target's vitality directly in real life.

When I didn't know what to say, the man grabbed my hand. His eyes were sparkling, like an explorer who'd just found an ancient treasure.

"This is it…this is what I've been waiting for! Ever since I saw the Headless Rider, I always wondered if this day would come for me…!"

"Huh? Huh?"

"Yeaaaaaah! I have no regrets!"

I had a bad feeling about this.

The desire within this man, which had seemed relatively ordinary up to this moment, suddenly surged, becoming vast beyond measure.

♂♀

"I've figured it out! It must be a Torch! No, a Mystes! Dammit, no wonder this demon of temptation looks so appealing! This is incredible—I bet there's a Tenmoku Ikko within me right now!"

What is he saying? I don't understand the meaning of these words.

Well, he's faced with a being that is utterly unfamiliar to him. Some confusion is to be warranted…but still, something's odd.

What human being would be able to accept this state of events so easily?

"A-at any rate, speak your desires, human, and envision it as strongly as you can within your mind. Is that understood?"

It was vague and fuzzy earlier, but as long as he was focusing on the image, I would have a much crisper idea of it. At that point, he would be mine. I would suck out his life!

The foolish lamb, with no idea that I meant to kill him, took me directly at my word.

Now go on. Speak your desire to me.

You will be dragged into your own thoughts, and drown in eternal pleasures…

"Then…then…I want Yomiko Togano to give me my own nickname! Like Schäferhund, or Glass Beast!"

"A nickname...? That is a very strange interest to have. Bah, very well...then summon the face and voice of this Togano to your mind, and... W-w-wait, what?"

Just as I hoped, his mental image was finally sharp and vivid. But what appeared was...

"Hurryyy! Hurryyy! Hee-hee-hee! I can't think of a more exciting honor than to be called a nickname by the witch herself!"

"Er...the only things I see in your mind are *text and illustrations*..."

"What?! Of course! Togano is a character in a book called *Missing*! Oh, or should I go with the manga version instead?! Oh, right! Her voice! Yes, of course, you'd want Makiko Ohmoto, who appeared in the radio drama version..."

"Wait! Hold on! Stop assuming I've already read this book you're talking about!" I shouted.

Undeniable shock and disappointment filled his expression. "Why haven't you read it?! Aren't you a succubus?! Aren't you drawn to human desires and wishes?! Aren't you basically a friend to Kageyuki Jinno already?!"

"I have no idea what that means!"

"I wanna be a motorrad and have a girl ride on my back."
"Please fall out of the sky and come to me."
"I want a thicc 2D girlfriend."
"I want to join the Knights of the Blood and befriend the vice commander."
"I want to be a Demon Lord and get a job at MgRonalds."
"I want to pilot my robot little sister."
"Please give me twenty thousand clone little sisters."
"Please give me a cute little sister who can't be this cute."
"I'm fine being an irregular, just give me a superior little sister."
"I just want a little sister...!"

The man continued to spout new desires left and right, but not a single one was something I could understand. For some reason, all of the images that came to his mind were flat two-dimensional drawings. It seemed that he could only envision things as comics or illustrations.

"I have no idea what you are talking about! If you want a younger sister, ask your parents! Face reality!"

"I am facing reality! I've got a succubus right in front of me!"

Damn. I've never come across anyone like him before.

Tokyo is a fearsome place... The freeloaders at the castle claimed that 80 percent of Japan was made of two dimensions... Is that really all there is in this country?!

"B-bah, I cannot deal with you!" I said. Something was eerie about the whole thing, and I made to leave the van.

"No you don't! You're not going anywhere!"

Damn! Such powerful desire! I feel as though I'm the one being sucked into him!

"I've finally got this great succubus! I'm gonna make you work for me!"

"Absolutely not! For one thing, I cannot convert two-dimensional images into three dimensions!"

"The cel shading tech in the game industry is unparalleled! They can do anything! My hopes were very slim before, but now I totally believe in them! I believe in dreams! I believe in hope!"

He grabbed me from behind and grappled me down, keeping me in place.

Shit! My stamina... My strength won't hold out.

It's all over. I spent too much of my power reading his mind.

My transformation...

It's going to be undone.

I'll look exactly the way I did when I left Germany...

Noooooooooooo...

When he saw my true form, the man across from me gaped with shock, and he pointed a finger.

"Oh...is that...?!"

♂♀

Back alley, Ikebukuro

...That was dreadful.

But at least I've recovered enough that I can hide my form from sight. Anything more than that, and I wouldn't be able to survive, so I got him to let me go... Imagine that—a succubus asking to be "let go"... Utter shame upon me!

...But then...that man never tried to take my clothes off. He just watched. I suppose that makes him something of a gentleman...?
No, no, no. Of course not. If anything, that's creepier.
Blast it, is there no ordinary person in this city?
Or have I just had the luck to catch sight of nothing but freaks?
That first boy was normal, though... Hmph. Whatever. I'll stay hidden this time and be very judicious in choosing my next victim.

I walked down an empty road and strove to recover my strength within the cold night wind.

I have time now. No human can see me like this.

Yes, that's right.
No human can lay eyes upon me.
Which raises the question...
What is this?

Why do I feel...against the back of my neck...this deadly black blade?

I had no idea what was happening. All I could do was slowly and carefully turn around.

Drunn.

An engine whinnied behind me.

It was a black motorcycle without a headlight, and sitting astride it, clad in a black leather suit...

...Well, it's not human...

This being wielded a massive scythe evocative of death itself and silently glared at me from a helmet that offered no glimpse at the inside.

"...What is this? The presence I sense from you...is not a vampire, that much I can say... But wait. I've felt this somewhere before..."

I searched back through my long past memory, recalling a time that I had met a fairy with a similar presence...

And then I trembled with fear.

"A...a dullahan?!"

No!

No, no, no!

The angel of death, the valkyrie in black—the condolence-giver whose blade could separate the soul from the body of not just humans, but even other demons and vampires! Why was it here?!

Well, it did explain one thing. A dullahan could use its shadow to sense me when ordinary human beings could not.

But beyond that...what about the carriage of bone and the headless horse?! I've never heard of a dullahan riding a motorcycle!

"Wh-why..."

Why is such a thing here, and why is it showing itself to me?!

The only thing I knew for certain was that angering it would easily be the end of me. My soul would be ripped out of the world itself.

Nobody really knew where dullahans took the souls that they had removed from the owners.

And not knowing was the true terror.

But as I quaked with fear, the dullahan did something rather strange.

She (as far as I knew, all dullahans took female form) pulled her scythe away from my neck and took out a PDA from around her torso. Then she typed some string of words into the device and held it out for me to see.

"*Sorry for startling you. I'm Celty, a dullahan. I live around here.*"

?

Why did she not simply speak to me?

A dullahan's head is always removed from its torso, of course, but that just means they carry it around...

That was when I realized that, aside from the PDA, she was not holding anything. The scythe was probably fashioned out of her own shadow. There was neither hide nor hair of it now.

"Did you...lose your head...?" I asked hesitantly, not wanting to anger her.

But the dullahan promptly typed, "*I'm embarrassed to admit it.*"

Something about the way that she communicated through text reminded me of the viscount in my hometown.

The moment I associated the reaper with him, I found that my fear lessened by several degrees.

The dullahan continued to type. "*I've been watching you for a while now. You tried to seduce my companions and suck out their life force, didn't you? You tried to take their lives.*"

Companions? What is she talking about? I have never attempted to absorb the vitality of a dullahan...

But, wait.

This dullahan's soul...

Oh, there's no mistaking it.
But I can't believe my eyes.
It's connected.
There is indeed a soul bond between that Mikado boy and this dullahan!
What does this mean? How can a dullahan and human be acquaintances...?

While I struggled to grasp the meaning of this revelation, she continued to type into the PDA.

"*While you may have failed every time, you have attempted to do harm to my friends and the place where I live.*"

"*And you must pay for that.*"

♂♀

Night, along Kawagoe Highway, top floor of apartment building

"Ah, welcome back, Celty. How was it? Did you find this succubus you were..."

Shinra's greetings fell short when he actually saw Celty.

It was indeed a woman in the usual black suit.

But there was one part that was very different.

"Celty, you..."

What Shinra saw was a woman's head with pristine, beautiful features.

"Shinra."

A voice as pure and clear as the face it came from filled the room.

But Shinra did not take this at face value. He recalled whom she had gone out to find today and came up with an answer on his own.

"Celty...is this the succubus's...?"

"Don't say anything, Shinra." Celty shook her head and took a step closer to Shinra. "Do you not like me with a head...?"

She looked almost afraid of his answer, so Shinra gave her one of his gentle smiles. He knew what she was doing and decided to be honest.

"How silly... What do I always say? It doesn't matter to me whether you have a head or not, Celty."

He stayed sitting in his chair, looking a bit unconvinced, however.

"...Did you decide to show me this illusion just to ask that question?"

Celty leaned forward and placed her hands on the table so that she was resting against it. She leaned over, putting her face closer to his, and whispered, "I wanted to pay you back."

"Pay me back?"

"Earlier you said to hit you—because it takes the place of a kiss, right?"

"That's not something you need to pay me back for."

Celty shook her head and leaned closer to him.

They could feel each other's breath at this distance.

"Yes, I know that. And I know that you love me without a head."

Although he knew it was an illusion, Shinra could feel Celty's breath on his skin.

"So this is my little whim," she said.

"Huh?"

He blushed like an adolescent boy. Celty gave him an impish little grin.

"I've already been dyed in the colors of this city. You might say that I have the heart of a true resident of this place. Or at least, that's what I wish. And can you tell what wish I asked the demon to grant?

"I want to kiss you. That is my desire."

♂♀

Apparently, it worked.

Once I saw the two locking lips in the window, I breathed a sigh of relief and headed off.

When that dullahan had rounded upon me, I was so certain that I was going to die—go figure that she was actually offering me a deal.

"You must grant my desire in exchange for my mercy."

I had no idea what she meant at the time, but once I peered into her mind, I was stunned.

Her wish was even more juvenile than that Mikado boy's. It was like something a child would wish for, but far stronger than anyone else's desire in this place.

But what an ironic twist it is!

Of all the people whose desires I could represent, the one whose wish was the purest and most potent of all was not actually human.

＊　＊　＊

In the end, I left without taking the life force of the dullahan and human man.

The effect of the illusion would last for a while longer, so he would be able to see her head all night long.

Until this moment, I had taken it upon myself to "interpret" the dullahan's voice for her, using the thoughts in her head—but no words would be needed anymore.

Lastly, I turned back in midair to glance at the dullahan with the watermelon on her neck.

The illusion was one thing, but to physically kiss her, there would need to be a solid object. The dullahan named Celty decided to place a small watermelon on her neck to be her head. The helmet would have been too big for the job, so she paid a visit to the nearby grocery store.

Personally, I was most shocked at the idea of a dullahan waiting in line and buying items in a store like an ordinary human being.

Still…a watermelon, huh?

Speaking of which, I wonder what that watermelon vampire is doing right now. Without me to provide the dreams, I have a feeling his transforming powers have been abused for that purpose.

Oh well. I suppose I could return to Germany for his sake. *Not* for the viscount.

This place does not suit me.

I've learned this lesson painfully well.

So if I'm going to leave, I at least want that dullahan to be happy, given that she's the only one with a proper desire—no, love—in this twisted place.

…It's all a big joke, isn't it?

I wonder what the viscount will say about this.

Me, a creature that devours human lusts, wishing for the happiness of another.

But…it does feel a little bit nice, I'll admit.

I must be hallucinating after going through such harrowing experiences. But at least it's a pleasant hallucination. It's worth enjoying.

Considering how this dullahan is surrounded by twisted human beings, as a fellow non-human—as a fellow woman, even—I chose to send her quiet well-wishes.

"…Sweet dreams."

* * *

I chuckled and turned away for good, extending my wings to their full length, and taking flight toward the place I truly belonged.

I was fully done with this city—but thanks to the dullahan, I found that I actually *liked* the place just a little bit.

I'm done with it for now, but maybe someday I'll return.

Everyone will be so shocked when they hear I know a dullahan now. Even the viscount will be shocked.

That's right. I'll come back for *that*.

And I'll bring everyone else from the castle with me…

♂♀

Ikebukuro

"What's up, Yumacchi? You seem in a really chipper mood."

"Heh-heh-heh-heh, can you tell? Aw, geez, I bet I'm shining so brightly, a reaper of souls might be coming to get me."

"Dressed all in white? Or the one delivering letters?"

"Uh, the creepy bubbly kind."

In the backseat of the van, Yumasaki had a strangely entranced look in his eyes. It was like he wasn't fully present, like he was awake and having a dream at the same time.

"You look happy, but also kinda sick."

"Huh? Oh, sorry about that, Kadota. I just got a bit of *life force sucked outta me*."

Karisawa and Kadota shared a look, trying to figure out what he meant by that.

But Yumasaki was still engrossed in the heaven he'd tasted recently.

I don't think they'd believe me, anyway.

The haggard succubus had shown its true self to him, a sight that he savored, replaying it in his head now.

Given the way it talked and the neutral-sounding voice, I thought the demon was a man… How could I have expected a babe like a manga character, with blonde hair and blue eyes—and a maid in green, to boot?!

"Hee-hee-hee-hee, hee-hee-hee-hee-hee-hee-hee-hee. Ahh, if only she were 2D, I would have proposed on the spot. Too bad, hee-hee-hee-hee-hee-hee."

"Ugh, you're being creepy, Yumacchi. Kino woulda shot you dead in no time…"

Yumasaki completely brushed off Karisawa, recalling his experience. "But I did draw a bunch of sketches so I can convert her to 2D. I'll need to ink those later…hee-hee-hee, hee-hee-hee-hee-hee."

"Has he completely cracked at last…?"

The other two looked at Yumasaki with suspicion, but he never wavered from the triumphant smile that stuck to his face.

It went on and on and on…
This is a fantastical tale.
A tale of a dreaming fantasy.

Fin

EPILOGUE, OR SIDE STORY 9
FESTIVAL SPIRITS

Festival day, Japan

The chants and strains of the festival music filled the night sky.

It was like the hearts and minds of the people in the streets were being reflected upward.

Even if not everyone on the streets was human, the festival music would envelop them all the same.

Wow...

With Celty's night vision, she could sense a couple enjoying a bit of a makeout session amid the trees off the path.

The headless woman hastily averted her "gaze" and typed up a message to show to Shinra.

"Being able to see in the dark is a double-edged sword. You end up spotting things you didn't need to see."

"What did you spot?"

"Nothing," Celty lied, strolling past the food carts with Shinra.

It would be crude to make light of other people's romantic lives. Plus, if I'm foolish enough to mention it, Shinra's going to say, "Let's go find our own dark spot and do that, too!"

They were at a festival being held near Ikebukuro. She was dressed in a black-themed kimono, while Shinra wore a yukata that was primarily white.

Few were surprised to see the dullahan out and about. In fact, almost no one looked at her with curiosity.

This was because she had removed her trademark riding helmet and disguised herself as a human today.

Now, the disguise in this case was simply extending her shadow to create a mass of long hair, then adding one of the typical anime character masks that were so often sold at festivals. It didn't seem that anyone who passed by her was interested in what was under the mask; it meant she could stroll in peace and be one with the crowd, and no one was any the wiser.

"*It really is crowded, though. I haven't been through a crowd of this size since I made that delivery at the summer event to Yumasaki and Karisawa.*"

"All the festivals in Tokyo are crowded. The Fukuro Festival in Ikebukuro brings tons of attention and life to the area right by the station."

"*That's true. I've passed by there when it's on… It's a really wild festival.*"

This festival was not on the same scale, but it still featured an impressive array of food and entertainment, and the lively excitement and atmosphere was as thrilling as any other event.

"Let's just enjoy the evening! I'll show you all the things there are to do, aside from just eating food!" Shinra said, grinning like a child. Celty's fake, masked head nodded.

♂♀

The first stand they saw that offered something other than food was an old-fashioned shooting gallery.

"We have to try shooting first, Celty! We'll take one go, mister!" Shinra said, paying the man behind the counter. He handed Celty a toy gun, much to her confusion.

"Hang on, young lady, are you really going to aim that with your mask on?" the man asked. Celty tilted the mask without a word, then took aim with the gun.

Heh-heh-heh. I know how this works from movies and comics. They always have supports holding up the really expensive items, so they don't actually fall over. It's just the sort of thing a real trickster would think up. But I'll play along and give it a try at first.

She pointed the gun at the alarm clock on the highest pedestal and fired.

A burst of air.

The cork shot forward.

The projectile flew at the clock on the highest point, hitting the target—and with a heavy lurch, the clock wobbled and toppled right off the shelf.

Huh?

"Congratulations!"

Huh? Huh?!

"That was impressive, young lady! You knocked the alarm clock clean off!"

To Celty's shock, the people around her started to applaud.

Shinra was beside himself with excitement. He hugged her shoulder to him and shouted, "Amazing, Celty! You got it in one! It's because you're always thinking such good thoughts!"

Even the man running the game had to give it to her. "Well, I'm out a lotta money for that one, but at least it went to a charming girl like you, eh?" he said with chagrin.

She felt very self-conscious about it.

No, I…I just assumed you were a cheat… I called you a trickster in my mind…

"So happy you can't even speak? Well, that just makes my day. Go on, take your prize!"

She took her alarm clock and walked a short distance from the game stand.

"That was incredible, Celty! It's more than just beginner's luck! You must have a real talent for shooting games!" Shinra said, excitedly heaping praise onto her. Her shoulders slumped.

I feel ashamed of my cynicism… I wish I could bury myself in a hole right now…

"Why are you so depressed?!"

I'm sorry, Mr. Shooting Gallery Man… I'm sorry!

♂♀

Once Celty had recovered her mood, they moved on and tried their luck at other festival games like the ring toss, darts, mold carving, and bouncy ball scoop.

Either through good luck or Celty's innate good skill, she won game after game until she was carrying a pile of prizes around with her. It put her in such a good mood that she was looking left and right like an excited child.

"What do you think? Is the festival fun?" Shinra asked.

"Yeah, I think so. It's much more fun than I thought it would be. Everyone else is having fun, too... The crowds here feel completely different from the usual crowds around town."

"That's true. Despite all these strangers, the strains of the festival music around you brings us all together, sharing this experience. That's a really special thing."

"...Yeah."

Especially when it's with you.

"Were you just thinking, 'Especially when it's with me'?"

"No, I wasn't! Don't get full of yourself!" Celty lied, to hide her shock at his good guess. At that moment, they came across a mask vendor. *"Oh, they have proper masks here too,"* she noted, seizing on the opportunity to change the subject.

"Yeah, we just bought that mask you've got at a variety shop. You want to get a new one and switch it out in the shadows?"

"Yeah, that's not a bad idea...and I don't want to wear the same mask the entire time," Celty replied, making her way to the mask seller—but she had difficulty believing what she saw there.

Dominating the upper half of the six rows of masks on sale was a design that was clearly based on the full-face riding helmet that Celty typically wore.

Huh?

...Wait, what?!

She did a double take. Even Shinra was shocked by it.

"What?! What are these masks, old lady?!"

"Oh, sonny, you should call me *young* lady instead, hee-hee-hee!" cackled the woman, who was in her fifties or sixties. She grabbed one of the Celty's-helmet-styled masks and put it on as a demonstration. "This is a mask of the latest crazy in Ikebukuro, the Headless Rider. Not that it makes much sense to have a mask of a headless creature. Hee-hee!"

Her cackling had a weird, high-pitched quality to it.

"This is horrible," murmured Shinra. "They've turned you into a product to sell, Celty..."

"Let it go, Shinra," she typed. She was just as shocked and confused,

but she felt that keeping Shinra calm was for the best. But before she could show him the message, Shinra pulled his wallet out.

"So I might as well buy it! I'll take all of them!"

"What are we supposed to do with these...?"

Celty made a sighing motion, laden with the alarm clock and other prizes, on top of a huge number of masks. Because she was wearing one of the masks modeled after her own helmet, it kind of just looked like the normal Celty from a distance.

"Sorry, sorry. Couldn't help myself... Hang on, I'll carry those, Celty."

"They're not heavy or anything..."

"Go on, go on. Let's take a little break."

He practically grabbed the items from her, then walked her over to a stone step slightly removed from the row of stands.

"If only they were doing a fireworks show, too. Apparently that's not part of the custom for this festival."

"Oh, I see. That's too bad," Celty replied.

Shinra suggested, "I don't have any particular plans for this trip we've got coming up, so do you want to go see the fireworks show in Akita on the way?"

"That would be nice. I want to see fireworks somewhere other than Sumidagawa for once."

"The Omagari Fireworks Show is supposed to be grand."

The tipsy feeling of the festival had them talking about their future plans. It was at this point that Celty realized *they* were one of the couples keeping its distance from the crowd now. She thought back to the couple she'd seen making out earlier.

Ugh, what am I thinking?! I wouldn't dare do something so embarrassing with all these people around! she thought, and glanced at Shinra.

Illuminated by the festival and looking up into the sky, Shinra's smile made him look like an eager child.

"But even without fireworks, just looking up at the sky like this with you is all I need to be happy. I'm never bored."

"Shinra..."

Celty had been on guard, expecting that he would try to leap on her. His smile caught her by surprise. She felt guilty at having been cautious of him, but there was another emotion she felt toward Shinra that was flooding through her now.

Oh, damn. What do I say at a moment like this...?

If she were human, her cheeks would have been bright red. She wanted to figure out how to end this deadlock, to say something important to Shinra...

But someone else intruded on their moment, ruining it permanently.

"Hey, you."

Hmm?

"Yeah, you. Who said you could wear *my mask*, bitch? Huh?" said a strange man, to their surprise. Shinra and Celty just looked at one another in confusion.

It wasn't the nature of his accusation that surprised them, however, but his *appearance*.

"Huh...? Celty cosplay?"

......

"Hah? What are you starin' at, huh? Who said you could go around wearin' my mask on my turf? Speak up! Huh? Don't you think you owe me a li'l somethin' first?"

Something about the voice and the way he's threatening us sounds familiar, Celty thought nervously. She gave him a closer examination. *But it can't be...*

This large, muscular man, wearing the same kind of face-covering helmet and black riding suit as Celty, gloated stupidly. "Geh-heh-heh, I think you don't realize who you're talkin' to, so I'll give you an education! Have you heard of the fearsome Headless Rider? Because that's me—*rglfhbl!*"

Realizing that this was the very same Fake Shizuo who had appeared in Ikebukuro before, she did not hesitate to smash the would-be extortionist.

He collapsed, foaming at the mouth. She shoved her PDA in his face.

"Give back the money I gave you!"

♂♀

Despite some unforeseen incidents, Celty thoroughly enjoyed her first festival experience.

But as with all enjoyable things, it had to come to an end.

After ten o'clock, the stands began to tear down and pack up.

The crowds thinned out into a trickle, and the particular sounds unique to a Japanese festival steadily dwindled to nothing. The only thing left was a very minimal amount of music, muted to avoid bothering the neighborhood.

As the workers dismantled all the stands in the distance, Shinra and Celty stayed where they were. The festival's end was keen in her senses, and so was a feeling of loss.

Aww, it's ending. The festival is over, she thought.

"Hey, Shinra.

"Let's come back to the festival again…next year."

"Celty…"

She hoped the words would ease the sense of loneliness she was feeling. Under the warm light of the paper lanterns, Shinra gave her a comforting smile.

"Of course we will. Anywhere you want to go, I'll be there with you."

He was the same Shinra as ever.

But when the same words were said in this special situation, they filled her with a strange and awkward self-awareness. Unable to shake the sensation, she reached for Shinra's hand.

…Thank you, she wanted to type with her free hand, but instead, she stopped and allowed herself to do nothing more than hold Shinra's hand.

He said nothing either, and clasped it gently back.

And on, and on, and on.

Until the sounds of the festival subsided at last.

♂♀

"The time spent in a festival always feels short.

"But if you include the days we spend looking forward to them, the life we spend with them is very long indeed."

She couldn't remember what the TV show was about.

But Celty could still clearly hear that narration. The phrase echoed in her head, and she had to agree with it.

I just can't wait for the next festival to arrive.

But as long as I'm with Shinra, I know it will be a pleasant wait.

Maybe it just feels so short because I had so much fun.

Celty had been alive for a long, long time, so there were times that a year felt short to her.

But she also was keenly aware that Shinra's time was limited.

There was no telling how many years they would have after this.

That was a sobering fact for Celty, but she enjoyed her festival as though it were the only thing that could clear away those clouds.

Because their time together was limited, the memories they did create would be forever etched on their souls.

Celty let the music of the festival color her heart.

As if to say that the festival of life had only just begun.

And praying that in their time together, they would hear many more festival chants in the years to come.

AFTERWORD

Hi, it's been awhile. I'm Ryohgo Narita. I doubt that very many of you will be reading *Durarara!!* for the very first time in this collection of side stories, but if that happens to be you—welcome! I recommend saving this afterword until you've finished reading the entire book, because I will touch on some spoilers!

Yes, it's a side story (or several)! It's a festival! The *Durarara!!* series ended with the thirteenth volume and continues in the *Durarara!! SH* series with the same setting and a mostly new cast, but since this year, 2014, is the tenth anniversary of *Durarara!!*, we decided to gather some of the shorter pieces I've done over the years into their own collection!

Many of these are from the *Dengeki Bunko Official Bootleg* series, which are primarily parodies, so they feature more satirical and meta content than the usual *Durarara!!* Since this is a bit of a "festival" book to celebrate the tenth anniversary, I hope you'll enjoy them for what they are.

SIDE STORY 1: HOT LIKE THE POT OF MY SOUL
This story ran in *Dengeki Bunko Magazine*. I decided to take the hot pot party that appeared briefly in the main series and expand on it. Various details from the characters' pasts are revealed here. It's even got some details I probably should have written into the main series, such as Shizuo and Tom's first meeting, and Mika and Anri's. After checking out Mikado and Masaomi's start, you might find that a re-read of Volume 13 brings you a different flavor.

SIDE STORY 2: DUFUFUFU!!
A short story with an "impostor" theme from the *Official Bootleg* series.

I didn't actually think that the premise of a fake Shizuo would fill out an entire short story. Just goes to show what can happen if you give it a shot. The voice actor references from Yumasaki and Karisawa were a little too pointed originally, so I pared them down a bit for this release. It's the kind of reference that someone who doesn't watch anime would never get anyway.

Of course, if this inspires you to check out the animation or games that these wonderful actors voice, that would be best of all! Yes...we have the second season of the anime going, and they recorded extra lines for the *Durarara!! 3way standoff -alley-V* port on the PS Vita, so check it out! (#shill)

SIDE STORY 3: BESPECTACLED BEAUS: THE DOUBLE SHOTGUN

A brief piece around Karisawa's daily life, from the *Official Bootleg* series. I'm glad I was able to demonstrate that Karisawa *does* have friends outside of the van gang. Hopefully I'll have a chance to shine the spotlight on her friends at some point in the future.

SIDE STORY 4: *DURARARA!!* TRUE STORIES: THEY GET ALONG
SIDE STORY 5: *DURARARA!!* TRUE STORIES: THEY GET ALONG 2

On the shelves for Dengeki Bunko releases at the bookstore, you may have seen the plastic dividers that stick out between certain authors or series so they're easier to find. As a matter of fact, these stories were written specifically to be printed on the *Durarara!!* series dividers if you pull them out. But some people order their books online, or their local store doesn't have dividers, so I always hoped I'd be able to run them in a short story collection at some point. I'm glad that moment has arrived.

SIDE STORY 6: *DURARARA!!* X√20 THE COMING-OF-AGE COMES AT ONCE

Another *Official Bootleg* story, this time themed around "what if they were twenty years old...?" I think the idea was that it would be about young teens or child characters as they turn into adults, but I failed to pick up on that, and I wrote about my adult characters reminiscing on their coming-of-age ceremony instead.

SIDE STORY 7: NICOCOCO!! (*NICONICO NOVEL* SHORT-TERM SERIAL)

This was an online story serialized in the *Official Dengeki Bunko Blog-Magazine* on the Niconico website over four weeks, collected into one piece. There are some references to the way that Niconico works, and as I wrote it, I was marveling over how much the Internet has changed in the last ten years. If Niconico and Twitter had existed when I was writing the first volume of *Durarara!!*, it might have turned into a completely different story.

SIDE STORY 8: *DURAMP!!* AVOIDING LOVE IN THE CENTER OF THE WORLD

This story was from a much older *Official Bootleg* issue. As I wrote in the intro to the story, this one features a number of references to my other series, *Vamp!* As a matter of fact, I also have another *Official Bootleg* crossover written from the perspective of the *Vamp!* series, which I hope I'll be able to show you one day.

Well, I'm out of time, so here are the usual acknowledgments.

Because many of these little stories are parody-centric *Official Bootleg* material, there are many more of Yumasaki and Karisawa's references than usual. I would like to apologize to, and thank, the authors of the various works that were obliquely mentioned for allowing me to indulge!

To my editor, Mr. Papio Wada, and everyone else involved in the production of this book.

To Suzuhito Yasuda, who brought our tenth anniversary to life with beautiful illustrations.

And most of all, to all you readers who came along for the past ten years and this year's festival.

Thank you all so much!

Ryohgo Narita, July 2014